"That's why you want this military contract.

"To help men and women like your father so maybe they won't pull away from the world."

"Like my father." Ruby nodded. "And my high school boyfriend. He came back so angry—not the same boy I knew at all. He's in prison now."

And that, Aaron realized, was exactly the path he'd been on. Hiding from the world and wallowing in his pain, both internal and external.

"Service dogs really do make a difference," she said, pulling herself back together. "I know they do. I've worked with many injured clients in the past, although you're my first marine."

"Don't hold that against the marines," he joked, trying to tease a smile from her.

It worked. Her radiant smile lifted both her countenance and his.

"I've said this before, but if you really try and work this program, Oscar may make all the difference in the world to you."

But at the moment, *Ruby* was the one making the real difference in his life…and Aaron wasn't about to say that out loud.

A *Publishers Weekly* bestselling and award-winning author of over forty novels, with almost two million books in print, **Deb Kastner** enjoys writing contemporary inspirational Western stories set in small communities. Deb lives in beautiful Colorado with her husband, miscreant mutts and curious kitties. She is blessed with three adult daughters and two grandchildren. Her favorite hobby is spoiling her grandchildren, but she also enjoys reading, watching movies, listening to music (The Texas Tenors are her favorite), singing in the church choir and exploring the Rocky Mountains on horseback.

Books by Deb Kastner

Love Inspired

Rocky Mountain Family

The Black Sheep's Salvation
Opening Her Heart
The Marine's Mission

Cowboy Country

Yuletide Baby
The Cowboy's Forever Family
The Cowboy's Surprise Baby
The Cowboy's Twins
Mistletoe Daddy
The Cowboy's Baby Blessing

Visit the Author Profile page at Harlequin.com for more titles.

The Marine's Mission

Deb Kastner

LOVE INSPIRED
INSPIRATIONAL ROMANCE

LOVE INSPIRED®
INSPIRATIONAL ROMANCE

Recycling programs
for this product may
not exist in your area.

ISBN-13: 978-1-335-56708-6

The Marine's Mission

This is a work of fiction. Names, characters, places and incidents are either the
product of the author's imagination or are used fictitiously. Any resemblance
to actual persons, living or dead, businesses, companies, events or locales is
entirely coincidental.

This edition published by arrangement with Harlequin Books S.A.

For questions and comments about the quality of this book, please contact us
at CustomerService@Harlequin.com.

Love Inspired
22 Adelaide St. West, 40th Floor
Toronto, Ontario M5H 4E3, Canada
www.Harlequin.com

Printed in U.S.A.

Let Israel hope in the Lord:
for with the Lord there is mercy,
and with him is plenteous redemption.
—*Psalm* 130:7

To Marcus Collins of The Texas Tenors:
I was listening to your solo album cover of
"You Needed Me" as I was finishing this book
and realized just how perfect a theme it was
for my characters. I'm so grateful for the
blessing of your talent and music
being shared with me and the world.

Chapter One

"You should probably know I don't want to be here."

Those were the first words United States Marine Corps Sergeant Aaron Jamison blurted out to the ginger-haired woman who'd just approached him, welcoming him with a pretty smile and an enormous, dorky-looking black standard poodle standing at her side, both with curious gazes. As far as Aaron was concerned, her choice in froufrou dogs obviously said a lot about her, kind of like the movie stars who carried tiny pups around in their purses to show off to everyone.

This was the breed of dog she'd chosen to own, and she was supposed to be an expert? She was going to be his service-dog trainer, put him through the program, and his first impression was she was probably as fluff brained as her dog, not someone he wanted to be in charge of him. He'd been told to meet up with Ruby Winslow, his new contact at A New Leash on Love, and since she was standing out here in front of the building, waiting for him, he assumed this was she.

In general, he didn't say much, and yet this time the moment he had stepped out of his truck, he'd put his foot in his mouth.

Two feet, even.

He'd blabbed exactly what had crossed his mind, and it wasn't the greatest beginning for either of them.

Neither did it bode well for him when she immediately stopped in her tracks fast enough to make the dust cloud around her cowboy boots, sparks snapping in her light blue eyes as her gaze narrowed on him and her smile wavered. The black poodle stopped with her and stared up at her, curious as to her sudden halt.

He'd rented a truck from Denver International Airport to drive into the Rocky Mountains up to the small town of Whispering Pines, where Winslow's Woodlands and the military service-dog program were located. The whole time he'd been thinking about how much he was going to hate the next four weeks and how he would rather be anywhere but here.

Every second was bound to be painful, both physically and mentally.

But in hindsight, he probably shouldn't have said as much aloud, at least not until after they'd been formally introduced.

Ruby looked as if she were about to reply to his rude comment, but then she pinched her lips together, took a deep breath and apparently thought better of it.

"I just thought you should know," Aaron continued, attempting to wind his way out of the knot he'd just firmly tied around his neck, "that although I have been given orders to show up and complete this program, I'm not exactly a willing participant here."

He was a straight shooter, both literally as a sniper in Afghanistan and figuratively in the way he lived his life in and out of the marine corps. He didn't say much, but when he did, he meant whatever words crossed his lips.

That said, he didn't want to start a war with Ruby this early on in his new mission, even if what he spoke was the truth. He *wasn't* here because he wanted to be. He didn't even really want a service dog, although he wasn't completely opposed to a tough-looking canine companion—a German shepherd, maybe, or a Belgian Malinois.

Not that what he wanted had ever once played into the situation. It didn't. Not from the beginning. But that didn't stop him from feeling angry and frustrated just thinking about having to endure the Veterans Administration's direct orders. Of all the veterans they could have selected for the program...

Why him?

Under duress was a mild way of putting what he was feeling right now. The VA was offering him up like a chimp in a laboratory just because of the specific injuries he'd endured while fighting for his country.

Troubled, painful breathing from the IED explosion sometimes caused him great pain and loss of balance. A traumatic brain injury often left him confused. His left leg had the tendency to drag with every single step if he wasn't always on top of it and was consciously paying attention to exactly how he was walking.

The IED hadn't even been the worst of his problems. External pain, he could deal with. It was coming back to a civilian life where no one understood what he'd been through that really got him. He'd never felt so alone.

Only his brothers and sisters in arms and other veterans understood his struggles.

And he wasn't into sharing.

He met the woman's eyes again and maintained his stiff parade rest posture, his hands locked behind him, not quite willing to take back his words even though he knew he probably should.

"I see," Ruby said, her voice calm and her tone low, though it didn't match the expression on her face at all. Her cheeks had turned as red as her hair, and he suspected steam was about ready to pour out of her ears. She'd no doubt screech like a boiling teapot if she didn't take a breath soon. "Why did the VA send *you*, then, Aaron, if I may ask? Didn't you agree to the specifications in our contract? I was quite detailed in what I asked for, and I thought the VA had agreed to my terms."

He shrugged and nearly groaned with the excruciating twinge the movement caused him. Pain had doggedly followed him around ever since he'd returned stateside, and he refused to take the pain medicine the doctor offered. His mind was cloudy enough without adding to the problem. Usually, he ignored whatever discomfort he endured, but with the extra stress today's situation was causing him, his agony came through loud and clear on his internal radio.

When a marine under his command had stepped on a mine while on patrol, he'd thrown himself on top of the man, saving the marine's life but putting a bitter end to Aaron's military career. Doctors had managed to remove most of the shrapnel from his body but couldn't do anything about the pain that haunted him. His lungs burned with every breath, often leaving him light-headed and throwing off his balance.

And that, he knew, was why the VA had thought he was the perfect guinea pig for their *pet project*, pun unfortunately very much intended. Apparently, a service dog was supposed to help him with those things, although he couldn't really see how. The only dogs with whom he was familiar were the biting and bomb-sniffing kinds.

Instead of answering Ruby's question out loud, he turned and walked about five feet, purposefully dragging his left leg, and then returned to her side, his breath coming in ragged gasps and his jaw so tight it was giving him a headache.

Ruby frowned, but not at him. He could see the wheels in her mind turning as she brushed her bangs out of her eyes with the back of her hand.

"And I understand your breathing and balance were also affected?"

Obviously.

"I'm sorry, ma'am, but if they already told you all this before I arrived, why are you asking me?"

Frustration, an all too familiar emotion, mounted again. He didn't like anyone focusing their attention too closely upon him, especially not a pretty woman, and he really hated talking about his injuries when he clearly didn't need to, since Ruby had been given a full report regarding his condition. His injuries were what they were. The IED had quite literally blown up his career in the marine corps. What was the point in talking about it?

"I would rather hear it from you. And don't call me *ma'am*."

He jerked his chin in agreement, although why this would be an issue with her was beyond him. He was just trying to be polite.

"I'd like to get your take on how you view your injuries and how exactly you believe a service dog might assist you. Before we get started, I need to find out what it is you'd like to accomplish from this program."

"To tell the truth, I don't understand how

a service dog is going to help me at all. It seems rather pointless to me. But if you want to know what I really want, ma'am, it's to get my dog and get out of here," he suggested with a wry twist of his lips.

"Okay. Well, we agree on that, although it's a little more complicated than a grab and go. Four solid weeks of training and a final test is involved before you and your dog will truly be a team. Why don't you follow me to my office so we can discuss the basics?"

Basic training. Great.

All the years he'd spent in the marines, serving his country and making career-killing sacrifices, and he was back to basic training. He wanted to turn around right now, get back in his rental dual-cab pickup truck and drive as far and fast away from here as he could. But as much as he wanted to, he didn't balk. Instead, he gritted his teeth and followed behind Ruby Winslow and her froufrou dog.

She led him past an outdoor training area containing a number of jumps, seesaws, tunnels and more—everything he imagined would go into training his service dog. He'd watched military dogs run through agility courses before. That part he was excited about. He could easily picture himself and his muscular German shepherd or intense Belgian Malinois running the course at lightning speed—well, at least the dog would be fast.

Him, not so much. The very thought of running made his lungs sting as if he were breathing daggers.

In another large fenced-off pen, at least a dozen dogs of various sizes and breeds were running around playing on a huge grassy area, wrestling with each other or nipping at each other's heels. Others were stretched out, comfortably resting under the shade of well-placed evergreens and aspen trees.

Ruby led Aaron into a rectangular building nearly the size of a football field. It was so large their footsteps echoed. As he entered, he was surprised to find it was a single concrete-floored room. Various leashes and other training paraphernalia hung on walls or were neatly organized on multiple shelving units.

In the far corner of the room was a single wooden desk and a half-sized filing cabinet with a printer on top of it. Again, everything appeared well structured. A large computer monitor took up most of the desk area, along with two filing baskets containing folders and a few loose papers.

Ruby sat down behind the desk, her dog flopping down beside her chair as she gestured to the seat across from her.

"Sit. Please."

"I'll bet you say that a lot around here," he said as he gritted his teeth against his pain and sank into the black leather office chair, which was surprisingly comfortable. He leaned back and crossed his arms.

She looked up from the folder she'd been perusing, looking thoroughly stunned for a moment before his words finally hit their mark.

"What? Oh—right. *Sit.* Yeah, we do that a lot here." When she laughed, it was high, throaty and genuine, and suddenly Aaron realized it might be to both their benefits to try to make a new and better start with her. After all, it wasn't her fault he was here. As far as he knew, she hadn't specifically been the one to select him for the program.

That would be the military. *His* military.

"Back there," he started, taking a deep breath that shot pins and needles through his body and—ironically enough—helped him think more clearly, "when I first stepped out of my vehicle. That wasn't exactly an intro-duction, was it?"

"No." She met his gaze head-on, curios-ity twinkling from her light blue eyes. "No, it wasn't."

He searched for antagonism in her eyes but found none.

She put down the folder she'd been studying and turned her full attention on him, leaning her forearms on the desk to bring them a little closer.

"I'm Ruby Winslow, the full-time dog trainer here at A New Leash on Love. Please call me Ruby. I'll be your point person and trainer while working with you and your new service dog, and then at the end of our four weeks together, we will be reporting our results back to the VA.

"If all goes as well as I hope, A New Leash on Love will win a military contract that will both bolster our program here and hopefully help many more of your brothers and sisters in arms to receive service dogs to benefit their lives.

"My three sisters also help with service-dog training from time to time, and you'll often see one or the other of us—sometimes all of us at once—about town with our dogs, getting them used to different locations and distractions."

Aaron remained silent as she spouted out all this information. She'd suddenly opened up like a fountain, and he didn't want to immediately shut her down as he had earlier.

That, and there were just oh so many words.

He wasn't sure if and when she wanted him to respond.

It took him a moment to realize she'd stopped talking and was staring at him, her eyebrows raised and her chin lightly tilted.

Had she asked him a question?

"What do you prefer I call you?" she asked in her soft, sweet tone. She was clearly repeating herself.

Yep. He'd missed a question, all right.

"United States Marine Corps Sergeant Aaron Jamison is a bit of a mouthful," she continued when he didn't answer.

He frowned. For almost his entire adult life, he'd been *Sergeant* to the people who mattered most to him. He'd never even considered what he was supposed to be called to those he'd meet now and in the future.

"Just call me Aaron," he finally said, cringing inwardly. His name sounded so—*barren*. Pathetic. Useless. It didn't say anything about him at all.

But it would be equally unworkable for her to use any other name. His marine corps career was behind him, and it was about time he faced the wretched future in front of him.

"Okay, Aaron. Are you ready to meet your new service dog?"

Aaron grinned. He'd always preferred action over speaking or paperwork, and he was anxious to see the dog with whom Ruby had paired him. "Now you're talking."

"Great," Ruby said, walking around the desk and leading the poodle at her side toward him.

"Aaron, meet Oscar, your new best friend."

Ruby wasn't altogether surprised when Aaron gaped. She was fairly certain he hadn't expected this particular turn of events. The rough-edged marine sergeant being given a standard poodle was, in a way, somewhat laughable. But Ruby had been working with service dogs for well over a decade and knew exactly what she was doing. She'd given a lot of thought to which of her dogs would be appropriate for Aaron and his specific physical issues, and Oscar was perfect for what he needed.

Aaron was just going to have to deal. He was the key to her receiving a military contract that might make or break their program's ability to continue, and she wasn't going to back down just because he didn't happen to like her methods.

Still, she had to admit she was already somewhat discouraged by their meeting. Usually, clients arrived excited and eager to train.

But the one time she needed cooperation, it appeared as if she wasn't going to get it. Unless she could change his mind.

"Oscar will be perfect for your needs," she assured him, reaching down to scratch the poodle's head.

"That froufrou dog? No way, ma'am. Not gonna happen."

"Excuse me?" She'd expected him to hesitate but not downright reject her idea.

"Look, Ruby, if you like Oscar so much, then keep him for yourself. I need a man's dog by my side, not some…some…"

"Poodle?" Ruby suggested, her eyebrows disappearing beneath her long ginger bangs. She could either get angry or laugh at the situation, and she'd always been prone to the latter, as difficult as it was for her now.

"Right. Whatever. Lead me to where you keep the German shepherds and I'll pick one out myself."

"Hmm," Ruby said, rubbing her chin as if considering his request, although she really wasn't. At length, she shrugged. "No."

"No?"

That obviously wasn't the answer he wanted to hear nor what he'd expected her to say. He was clearly used to giving orders, not taking them. He was gritting his teeth so hard she could see his pulse pounding in the corner of his scruffy jaw.

"No," she repeated firmly. "First off, we don't currently have a German shepherd as part of our program, much less several from which to choose. Nor do we have any Mals, before you ask."

She didn't tell Aaron that if she'd truly believed a GSD—German Shepherd Dog—or a Belgian Malinois would be the right breed for him and his circumstances, she would have searched the local shelters high and low and reached out to her contacts to find one. No use adding fuel to the fire.

"I'd even take a pit bull." He was beginning to sound desperate.

Ruby had a wonderful brown-and-white-spotted pit bull named Tugger currently on her program roster, but he definitely wasn't the right dog for Aaron. Just the way the marine had said he'd *even* take a pit bull told her all she needed to know on that subject.

"Nope. Nope. And nope. Look, Aaron. Either you're going to have to learn to trust me and my judgments where my specialty and training with service dogs are concerned or you may as well just leave now before we start. I don't have any inclination to constantly knock heads with you at every turn. This isn't going to work unless you're ready to listen to me and do whatever I tell you to do."

His eyebrows furrowed. "I understand chain of command, ma'am. There were many times as a marine when I didn't exactly agree with my superiors, but I understood why it was important to follow orders."

"Okay. I guess that's one way to look at it. Let's go with that."

Talk about making her uncomfortable. She'd always considered herself a teacher and not so much a leader, especially the type this military man was used to obeying. She couldn't even imagine running a boot camp here and barking—pun definitely intended— out orders at him, and yet she suspected that was exactly what Aaron thought he was about to experience.

"For me," Aaron continued, standing, "following orders is black and white. My marines' lives under my command often depended on it. But as you can see, I'm having difficulty making that transition in this situation. We're not talking people's lives here."

"I disagree. We're very much talking lives—*yours*. You may not yet have a clear vision of what you'll be able to do with Oscar, but a service dog can make all the difference in the world."

"Yes, but you just insisted the best dog for me is a *poodle*. I'm sorry, but that can't be right. If you knew anything about me at all, you'd know the last dog in the world I'd choose would be a poodle."

"And yet I still believe I'm right," said Ruby with a wry smile. She couldn't back down now. Somehow, she had to convince this man she knew what she was doing. Internally, she was sweating. "I carefully studied your file before you arrived, Aaron, and specially selected Oscar for you to work with. I'm the expert here. So how are we going to get over this hurdle?"

"I have orders from the VA to make this work. How will it look to them if I turn back so quickly and give up before I even start the process?" He shook his head. "No. Don't answer that. It will look as if I wasn't able or competent enough to complete my mission. That's never going to happen. I'll *always* pull through, no matter what the circumstances."

Ruby was having difficulty considering her working relationship with Aaron a *mission*, but then, that was probably the only worldview the tough marine knew. She realized she'd do better to speak to him in terms he could comprehend and act upon.

"I'll do my best to work with you in a way you understand," she promised him. "In terms of giving orders and such."

That's what she did with her dogs, after all. Looked at each one as an individual and worked with them in a way they understood. Not that Aaron could even remotely be compared to her canines—except perhaps for the occasional bared teeth.

"This is my first time working with a military man, so give me some leeway."

That wasn't entirely accurate, and her gut squeezed painfully. She'd had experiences with military men before—both her father and her high school sweetheart, who'd returned from the Middle East troubled and with issues they ultimately couldn't overcome.

There was the irony. It was one of the primary reasons gaining this military contract was so important to her, and yet it was the very reason working with Aaron and others would be so difficult.

Her heart had already withstood so much. If it wasn't that the service-dog program was on the brink of folding, she might not have accepted the challenge to begin with. She believed with her whole heart that A New Leash on Love was a ministry to those it served. But even ministries needed funding, and hers was full of sweet canines who needed food and veterinary care.

It was worth it. But she had to dig deep to find the courage to confront her past and rise to face her future.

She believed she could help. But what could she do if Aaron didn't give her the opportunity to prove it to him?

"Look, ma'am," Aaron said, his jaw finally loosening as he moved out of parade rest. She shot him a look and he corrected himself. "Ruby, I mean. I never turn away from challenges. Not in boot camp, not in Afghanistan and not now, no matter how I personally feel about it. That's what makes me a good marine."

He paused and blew out a breath. "*Made* me a good marine," he corrected.

"'Once a marine, always a marine,'" she gently reminded him. "Right? I'm sure I heard that somewhere. Look—" she swiped a palm across her cheek "—if you're willing to push through the awkwardness, then so am I. I think—hope—you'll find it isn't as bad as you imagine it will be. Don't discount the training process. Who knows? You may even grow to like Oscar."

"I don't know about that, but despite my reticence, I'm willing to give it a go. Conquer this new terrain."

Ruby thought it was an odd way of looking at their working relationship. But then again, it kind of made sense to her, in a what-it-must-be-like-to-be-in-the-marine-corps kind of way.

She only hoped he didn't expect her to shout out orders like some kind of drill sergeant. That wasn't her teaching method and never would be. She believed in positive reinforcement both for her dogs and her clients and couldn't even imagine what it would be like to yell at someone. The man was troubled enough without her screaming orders at him.

She was the sweet talker in her family. Her wins came from her soft-spoken nature, while Aaron's, no doubt, were from a heart that was as rough and scarred inside as his outside. She couldn't even imagine what he'd seen and experienced, but she knew no one could walk away from such circumstances without it affecting them in some way.

That's how it had been for Daniel. She'd thought she'd be married with children by now. She and her high school flame had so many plans. And then he'd entered the army and come home…*different*.

Ruby was now more convinced than ever that Oscar would be the perfect service dog for Aaron, a dog who *wouldn't* constantly remind him of everything he'd been through. He'd probably had military-trained German shepherds and/or Belgian Malinois in his unit. Oscar was a sweet, even-tempered dog who could offer Aaron comfort and a sense of peace, maybe something he needed even more than the physical aspects of the work they would do together.

And maybe—just maybe— Ruby would be the right teacher for him, too.

Chapter Two

Friday afternoon was the first official training day for Aaron and Oscar, and Ruby had spent the whole morning cleaning the training building and worrying about how all this was going to turn out. Her sister Avery, who took care of the books for both the family companies, had shown her the latest numbers. Money was getting tighter and tighter.

She absolutely could not mess this up.

What had Ruby's contact, Major Bren Kelley, at the VA been thinking when she'd selected the sergeant as her test case? Aaron was *some* kind of case, all right, and Ruby wasn't at all sure what to do with him. She'd honestly expected a client who genuinely wanted to be part of the program.

Was that so much to ask?

Part of her wondered for a moment if perhaps Bren wanted her to fail, if she had something against a civilian receiving a military contract.

But no. Of course not. Ridiculous. That made no sense whatsoever.

The major had been the one to reach out to Ruby and A New Leash on Love after hearing of their success stories. This contract, *if* it came through based on the success of their first case together, would be mutually beneficial to both the veterans involved and the Winslows' training program.

It was a win-win.

Not only that, but it would be especially valuable to Aaron—if he would just open his mind and give it a chance. If he stubbornly dug in his heels starting on Day One, her military contract wouldn't have the opportunity to even so much as get off the ground.

Ruby sighed. Somehow, she very much doubted Aaron was going to give it his all, or even a little bit, if their first encounter was anything to go by.

He would be her most challenging client to date, bar none. Usually, people arrived at A New Leash on Love excited about meeting their new service dogs and looking forward to the journey of service-dog ownership and training. They were ready to listen and learn every step of the way. She hadn't the slightest idea how to even begin working with a client who didn't want to be here at all.

And yet, whether Aaron was willing to acknowledge his need or not, Ruby instinctively knew Oscar would be good for him. Over the years, she'd seen far too many clients' lives changed by a service dog to give up this early in the game.

And Ruby hadn't changed her mind on the breed of dog just because Aaron had pitched a fit about it. She had to admit she'd thought twice about it and then again some. The tension between her and Aaron might ease if she were to give in and switch to a dog that better fit Aaron's idea of what his canine ought to look like.

But there was so much more that went into the selection and training of a service dog than a particular breed looking *manly* enough for the tough marine who'd seen and experienced things Ruby could only imagine. If Aaron could stick with it, he would soon discover Oscar had special skills and abilities Aaron would eventually come to appreciate. If there had ever been a canine personality who could break down barriers, it was sweet Oscar.

Of course, that was *if* Aaron even bothered showing up for training on this warm Friday afternoon, and in Ruby's mind that was questionable. They were going to have to muddle through the next four weeks in each other's company. Ruby would do her best to help Aaron see his glass half-full and his service dog for what he was.

That was what Ruby did with all her clients—help them manage their physical and emotional symptoms and make their days bright. It was her ministry to the world and something she would never charge for, despite tight finances. A long-term military contract was different from helping individual clients, however, and was possibly the answer to her prayers.

"I'm here. Let's do this before I change my mind," came Aaron's deep, raspy voice from the door.

Ruby hadn't realized he'd been standing there. She glanced at her watch.

Five minutes early.

"Come on in. I'm glad to see you. Honestly, I thought you might not show. Or, at least, not show up on time," she admitted.

His brow furrowed as his chocolate-brown eyes caught hers. "What's that supposed to mean?"

She shrugged. "Just that you didn't appear

to be too thrilled about this whole operation yesterday when we first met. I didn't know if you wanted to participate."

"I don't. But that doesn't change anything. No one asked me what I wanted. They told me where to go and when to be there. My opinions have nothing to do with this." He paused and his gaze narrowed on her. "And I'm never late. *Ever.*"

Of course not. He wouldn't be.

"Great, then. Since you *are* here, let's go ahead and get started. First, I would like to exchange cell phone numbers with you. If at any point during your training you have a question or concern, feel free to reach out to me. Evenings and weekends are your special times with Oscar to relax and bond, but you never know when something might come up. And I'd like your number, as well, just in case I think of anything I need to add that can't wait until our next training day."

"Or to check up on me," he muttered under his breath.

Ruby chuckled. "Oh, definitely. That's what I meant."

She had no intention of using his cell number to check up on him, but he was so guarded about everything that she found it rather amusing.

"Today you're going to spend the day getting to know your dog," she told him. "Oscar, come."

His frown deepened when the black standard poodle with the teddy bear cut moved to Ruby's side and promptly sat in a heel position, his gaze focused on Ruby as he waited for his next command.

"Still a poodle?" he asked, annoyance in his tone.

She couldn't help but chuckle. "Last time I checked."

"I was hoping after we talked about it that you would reconsider and give me a different breed. Something more in line with my personality. Something *not* a poodle."

"I did reconsider. Carefully. But, Aaron, if this is going to work, you will have to trust me and the decisions I make for you. Starting now."

"Why should I?" His gaze met and locked with hers, a stubborn clench in his jaw. "I don't even know you."

Thankfully, she'd expected him to ask this question and was prepared with her answer.

"You've led men into battle because you knew what was best for them. You had knowledge and experience they didn't, and because of that, they trusted you enough to follow you. I'm asking you to do the same for me. Service dogs are my life, and I know what a difference Oscar can make in yours. No matter how you feel about it right now, I'm not going to steer you wrong here. That much I promise."

He stood stock-still for a moment. Ruby could practically see the thoughts whirring through his mind.

"What if I get to the end of training and still feel the same way about Oscar?" he asked bluntly.

She paused before answering. "Then of course you'll be free to leave without your service dog."

And the moment he walked away, her dreams of securing this military contract would be done for.

That couldn't happen.

This was everything to her, a way for her to help men and women who were like her father and Daniel. No one had been there to help them. Her father hadn't mentally recovered, and Daniel had ended up in jail.

She could make a difference. She knew she could.

"Do we have ourselves a deal?" Her mouth was so dry the words barely got past her lips.

She waited without breathing for Aaron to answer.

Finally, he shrugged, and his expression winced from the movement.

Aaron was hurting, and not just on the inside. Mentally and emotionally, too, no doubt. But Ruby had received his medical reports as part of the intake process. He still had shrapnel lodged where the military doctors couldn't remove it, which left him in constant pain, especially in his left leg, which tended to drag when he wasn't thinking about it. The explosion he'd suffered through made it difficult for him to breathe, as if he had asthma, and it also messed with his sense of balance. These were some of the specific reasons he'd been chosen to work with Ruby.

And this was also why Ruby hand-selected Oscar the standard poodle for the job and not a breed that would have been more acceptable to this rough-edged man's man. If any dog could reach through and heal this marine's shredded heart, it was Oscar.

"Okay, so let's get started, then," she said, grabbing a couple of fold-up chairs from the side wall and setting them face-to-face about four feet apart from each other. "Please, take a seat."

Without protesting for a change, Aaron settled in one seat while Ruby took the other. Ruby placed Oscar into a *sit* by her left side.

Aaron clenched his fists in front of him, unconsciously wringing his hands. He stared at Oscar as if he were the enemy, his gaze narrowed on the dog, unblinking. Aaron's muscles were so tight the tension was practically rippling off his shoulders and biceps. Head to toe, he looked as if he were a caged tiger ready to spring out the moment the door opened.

Ruby glanced down at Oscar, who— though he obeyed Ruby's sit-and-stay command and hadn't budged an inch—likewise looked ready to spring to life at Aaron's slightest movement. Dogs were better even than humans at picking up what people were feeling, and Oscar was an especially sensitive dog—which was part of the reason Ruby had selected him for Aaron in the first place.

But if Aaron couldn't calm his emotions and get a hold of his anxiety, what was supposed to be a relaxed and interesting first introduction was going to be a disaster. If Ruby could feel his irritation and indignation, then Oscar definitely could sense it.

"Aaron," Ruby said softly and evenly, drawing his gaze to hers, "I want you to take a deep breath and hold it for seven seconds, then exhale slowly."

"What?" he snapped, the unexpected sound causing Oscar to tilt his head and look at him in confusion.

"Inhale. Hold for seven. Exhale," Ruby repeated, following her own advice before she came completely unglued.

His brown eyes narrowed on her as he pressed his lips into a firm, straight line.

"Is this some sort of hocus-pocus woo-woo stuff you're trying to sell me here?" he asked suspiciously.

"'Woo-woo stuff'?" She couldn't help laughing.

"I'm serious," he said. "You ought to know up front I don't go for any of that junk. I'm a Christian."

"So am I."

He appeared so concerned by her suggestion to try breathing techniques that she reeled in her amusement so as not to offend him.

"The whole idea behind slowing your breath is to help you release the tension in your shoulders. You look as if you're about to pop up like a jack-in-the-box, and Oscar senses that stiffness in you. He's not going to interact well with you until you ratchet it down a few notches."

"Oh. I guess that's okay, then." He cleared his throat, straightened his shoulders and took the breath Ruby had suggested. "Better?"

"Much. Now, would you like to meet Oscar?"

"Not especially," he mumbled under his breath but loud enough for Ruby to hear.

Annoying man.

"Pretend you do."

His tension, which he'd managed to control only moments before, reappeared as if it had never escaped.

"Breathe," Ruby reminded him. Honestly, she couldn't understand why this was so hard for him, a brave marine who'd protected the United States by serving his country in far-off lands. And yet here he was, an innocent, fluffy dog clearly doing a number on him.

"Try this," she said, handing him a bag of liver treats.

He wrinkled his nose. "What's this for?"

"A snack." When he sniffed at the contents of the bag, she quickly added, "For Oscar."

His brow furrowed.

"To help him pay attention to you," she clarified. "I'm going to release Oscar from his *sit/stay*. When I do that, I want you to say his name. Be gentle but firm when you call him. Whenever he meets your gaze, praise him and give him a liver treat. You want him to respond to you and turn his attention toward you whenever you say his name. That's the first step in creating a strong bond between you."

"Got it," he said, digging inside the bag for a treat.

"Good. Oscar, release," Ruby said, allowing the dog the freedom to make this new choice on his own.

The dog stood and stretched one leg at a time, yawning widely.

"You're up," Ruby reminded Aaron.

"Right. Um… Oscar," he murmured hesitantly, in so light a tone that Ruby could barely hear him.

Thankfully, Oscar was fully trained and immediately responded to Aaron's vocal prompt, despite his utter lack of enthusiasm. The dog, at least, knew the point of the exercise.

"Once more with feeling?" Ruby suggested, hoping Aaron would finally take this seriously so they could get on with their training.

Otherwise, this was going to be the longest four weeks of her life. And if Aaron didn't put his heart into it, she might altogether be wasting time she could have been using to scramble for other ways to keep A New Leash on Love afloat.

For Aaron, the whole afternoon had been more agonizing than the Crucible at the end of marine boot camp, where every future marine spent fifty-four hours of sleep and food deprivation working operatives and marching nearly ten miles. Saying Oscar's name over and over and over again, with nothing to show for it other than a dog who would follow him around because he knew he had liver treats in his pouch was excruciating. Ruby instructed him to move to different parts of the giant room and call the dog by name, and then—as if that wasn't enough—he was expected to act as if Oscar had just won a prestigious award whenever the pooch came to him.

Ruby insisted he used high-pitched praise, despite how he choked on his own raspy voice. "Good boy, Oscar. Good boy."

Aaron could see the point of establishing a connection between man and dog, but that didn't make it any easier. He hadn't had any pets growing up and wasn't exactly comfortable ordering this dog around, however faithful he appeared to be.

Aaron felt kind of bad for Ruby, who was in charge of making this bond between him and Oscar work. Obviously, that was the first thing that had to happen before they could move forward with any of the other *stuff*. Unfortunately, he only had a vague notion of what that *stuff* might consist of, and on purpose or not, he was dragging his feet through the process. So far, all the surprises had been bad ones, and he wasn't looking forward to one minute of the next four weeks.

Oscar must be getting as bored with this whole process as he was, although the dog performed admirably and had boundless energy. Despite his personal feelings about the poodle, he could tell he was an intelligent dog who liked to work. He had to give the dog that much, even if he looked like the type of canine who had to go to the beauty parlor rather than the pet groomer.

"Bring it on in," Ruby finally announced, much to Aaron's relief. His leg was beginning to ache, and his lungs were screaming for a break and some fresh air. "Go ahead and take a seat while I grab Oscar's gear." She stood and headed to one bin-lined wall with several shelves placed above it. Everything appeared completely organized, and judging from the number of bins, there was a lot of it.

"'Gear'?" Aaron finally parroted. "You mean like his leash?"

"Yes, his leash, among other things. His service-dog vest. His feeding dishes, a bag of food, his grooming supplies and a couple of other goodies to get you by during your first few days together."

He sat down and she handed him a thick three-ring binder filled with information on how to care for Oscar full-time, around the clock, including having the dog sleep next to or preferably with him in his bed.

Was she serious? Didn't dogs belong outside or, at the very least, crated? Having never had a pet, never mind a service animal, this was all new to him.

He quickly perused a few more pages and furrowed his brow when he made another surprise discovery.

"Wait. You're expecting me to take him with me tonight? To the bed-and-breakfast where I'm staying?"

"Do you have any better ideas regarding how the two of you are going to bond? If so, I'm open to hearing them—but don't forget, I've been doing this for a long time with a great deal of success."

"Well, no. I guess not. I'd just figured we'd be training here every day."

"Oh, definitely. We will be. But during the evenings and on weekends when you're not with me, you'll have the opportunity to just hang out with Oscar and get to know him, and he'll learn all about you and your habits. The dog handlers in the military stay close to their dogs, don't they? If I'm not mistaken, they even sleep next to them, right?"

Aaron nodded but then slid his gaze over Oscar and cringed. "Yeah, they do. But those K-9s are working dogs. They're supposed to be ready at a moment's notice."

"Exactly. Oscar is a working dog who should be ready to come to your aid at a moment's notice. He just comes in a prettier package. You'll have to get used to the idea sometime. He can't help you if he isn't with you."

That was one mental block he would *never* get over. It didn't matter if the dog came in what Ruby termed a *pretty package*, or that his trainer likewise came in a *pretty package*. This was never going to work for him.

"What about Jake and Avery at the bed-and-breakfast? You're saying they won't mind me having Oscar along with me all the time?"

Ruby chuckled and Aaron's gut tightened. He was surprised by his reaction. He hadn't spent much time around beautiful women.

Sure, he'd had a few relationships over the years but nothing serious. He didn't believe his job lent to anything substantial or long-lasting. With him gone all the time, how fair would that be to someone? Ever since he'd been recruited into the marine corps right out of high school, it had been all work and no games. He'd been singularly focused on his job.

Now, when he suddenly didn't have any of those things to occupy his mind and his time, he found himself attracted to Ruby, especially when she smiled.

This wasn't going to do. He needed to focus on getting out of here in one piece.

"Avery is one of my sisters and is a big part of A New Leash on Love. She used to train dogs here, and she and Jake totally expect you to bring your service dog everywhere you go, including the B and B. They're completely on board with our program and will support you every step of the way."

"*One* of your sisters? How many sisters do you have?"

"Counting me, there are six Winslow siblings altogether. I have three sisters and two brothers. You've already met Avery, and I'm sure you'll meet the rest during your stay here. All of us work in one part of the business or another."

He whistled under his breath. He hadn't known many large families here in the United States, much less ones who worked together once they'd reached adulthood.

Ruby approached with a ten-pound bag of kibble slung over her shoulder. Aaron immediately stood to take it from her, but she waved him off. "Remember, I do this every day, most times with fifty-pound bags. This is nothing for me."

He could believe it. She was in excellent shape, no doubt from all the exercise she did with her dogs. Still, Aaron's male ego prompted him to want to help. It took all his will to follow her instructions. Reluctantly, he sat back down and crossed his arms, guessing the real reason she wouldn't allow him to help.

Because she saw him as weak, which really got his goat. As if his disabilities defined who he was as a man. He was positive she would have let any other man help her with her load. It was humiliating.

"Pay close attention to Oscar's nutrition," Ruby continued as she moved back to the supply station. "You'll be mixing fresh food with the kibble to make sure he gets everything he needs. Because he's a service dog, he needs to be in top condition, and high-quality food is an important part of his regimen."

Aaron grunted and nodded in agreement. It made sense. He kept himself in physical shape by weight lifting. A high-protein diet likewise played an important role in his conditioning.

"I get it. Diet and regular exercise are as important to working dogs as they are to humans. I work out."

He couldn't help but grin a little when her gaze swept over his chest and biceps and her eyes widened appreciatively, as did her smile.

His ego swelled a bit. He'd been taking hit after hit since his injury. He'd accept whatever admiration he could get, even in the middle of this surreal encounter.

Her cheeks turned a glaring shade of pink, clashing with her red hair as their eyes met and held for a moment before she cleared her throat and quickly turned back to Oscar. She picked up a large leather harness that looked to Aaron more like something a horse would wear than a canine and threaded it over Oscar's neck, adjusting the buckles so they fit snugly around his torso. The harness included a stiff handle that looked like something a blind man would use.

Once again, Aaron wanted to balk and head for the hills. This didn't feel right to him. He'd always been a fighter, but his flight instinct was on overdrive today.

"I don't want to look like a blind guy," he protested, not caring how unfeeling and insensitive he sounded.

"You won't. Not unless you're wearing sunglasses." She chuckled mildly at her own joke.

It wasn't funny. Not to Aaron.

She stood and stared at him for a moment with her hands on her hips as if she were deciding just how much she could expect out of him. "I think I see what the problem is here."

Really?

He was glad for that because he had no idea why he was reacting so differently and more insolently than he usually did. With all he'd faced in life, this should be a simple matter of conquering his own thoughts, as he'd done in basic training—and as with boot camp, his feelings should never, ever come out of his mouth.

"Enlighten me," he finally said.

"I'm only showing you this particular harness so you'll know it's available to use at appropriate times, such as when you go on a mountain hike. It's specially made for going up and down steep hills or walking on uneven ground. Oscar will help you with balance and forward momentum in situations like that. But I'll show you how to adjust this one later. Let's move on to another, the one you'll use in general situations."

She didn't even give him the opportunity to mentally switch gears before she had the leather harness off and was replacing it with a red nylon vest that was much simpler and more like Aaron had imagined a service dog's vest would look. It even had a patch on the side:

Don't pet me. I'm working.

"You can take this one back to the B and B with you tonight," Ruby said. "It's already adjusted for Oscar, so it's a simple slip-on, slip-off harness, over the head and clipped under the torso. He'll need to wear it whenever you are out in public. Whenever you put the vest on him, he'll know it's time to do his thing and will snap into work mode. But when you're home alone, it's fine to take it off so you and he can relax and bond. Do you want to try it on?"

He was about to shake his head but then caught himself and nodded. He could take apart a sniper rifle with lightning speed, and he quickly found he was equally as efficient at taking the service vest off the dog and putting it back on. Of course, it helped that Oscar cooperated.

"Why don't you walk Oscar around the building a few times to get the hang of it, and I'll load your supplies in the back of your truck."

"I can load my own supplies," he protested.

"Oh, I know. I'm not insulting you, Aaron. But right now, your primary job is to work with Oscar."

He was tired of being treated as if he couldn't do anything himself. It had been that way since the moment he'd been injured. Even in the hospital, the physical therapists had tried to take it easy on him. Little did they know how hard he would push to recuperate.

But today he didn't want to argue anymore, so he commanded Oscar to heel on his left side and walked around the outer perimeter of the building, getting used to gripping the harness and lead until Ruby was finished loading up his truck. He had to admit walking with Oscar really did have an effect on his balance, although it was too soon to know for sure how well that would work.

Since the weekend was now upon them and he wouldn't see Ruby until Monday morning, there was one more question he had before they were done for the day.

"You mentioned you're a Christian?"

"Yes. My whole family attends Whispering Pines Community Church on Main and Fourth. We take up nearly two whole pews now that my sisters are marrying off. You are welcome to worship with us. We'd be glad to have you."

"Thanks. I appreciate it. What time is the service?"

"Ten a.m. I'll watch for you so I can introduce you to the rest of us Winslows."

That sounded almost as overwhelming as having a standard poodle as a service dog, but he merely nodded his assent.

"Okay, then, you're set to go for the weekend. Like I said, Oscar knows he's working when he's got his vest on, so once you get back to your room at the B and B, you can take him out of his garb and just let him be a dog. For a service dog, being part of a family is just as important as the work he does. Let him hang out with you while you watch TV or whatever. Enjoy your Saturday with him, and I'll see you on Sunday at church."

Aaron felt silly even thinking about sitting on the couch cuddling with that huge ball of black fluff, but he didn't say so.

This was his load to carry, and he wouldn't walk away from it no matter how ridiculous he felt.

Worse things had happened to him. He could handle it.

It was only four weeks, after all. Four long and very painful weeks.

Chapter Three

Ruby showed up bright and early to church on Sunday morning, excited to find Aaron and introduce him to the rest of her family. They all knew a little bit about him, although she hadn't shared more than just the basics with them over dinner the evening before— that he was a wounded marine seeking a mobility assistance–service dog. Her siblings knew she'd purposefully chosen Oscar for the job and had been warned not to make a big deal over him, since Aaron was a little sensitive on the subject of being seen in the presence of a poodle—or a *froufrou dog*, as Aaron referred to him.

Being the one still in charge of the finances and paperwork for the family businesses in addition to working at her B and B, Avery was well aware of how important nailing this military contract was to Ruby and the continuation of the service-dog program, but they'd agreed to keep it between themselves for now. After all, if everything went as planned, there would be no reason to worry the rest of her siblings with the details.

As she did every Sunday, she'd selected one of the other service dogs in her program to bring along with her. Church folk here, including Pastor Aims, understood the importance of allowing service dogs in training to work in and experience all different types of situations and learn to guard against all distractions, and the Winslows' dogs were always welcome at the community church, as was anyone who was in need of a service dog themselves, as Aaron was.

Today she'd selected young, loving Tugger the pit bull mix, a special favorite of hers. She adored the way he always looked as if he was smiling, and his temperament was as sweet as his naturally upturned mug.

As she entered the foyer, she immediately looked around for Oscar. Aaron would be easy enough to spot as well, no matter what he happened to be wearing. He was tall enough to stand a head above most of the congregants and, though she wouldn't admit it to anyone but herself, catching his eye in any situation would surely make her heart swell.

But how could it not? He was a new guy in a town full of men with whom she'd grown up. Whispering Pines was a small town without a lot of eligible bachelors. Aaron was handsome in a rough kind of way and was a man who would catch most women's eyes. Why wouldn't she notice him?

Finally, she found him. He was standing stiffly in the far corner of the foyer all by himself, his arms crossed over his chest and gaze on the floor. It wasn't exactly a stance that welcomed people to approach him and introduce themselves, especially given his size, though she knew the people of Whispering Pines Community Church would look beyond that and offer their hands in friendship.

What she *didn't* see was Oscar.

Her gaze narrowed on Aaron, and she pressed her lips together. What had he not understood about her instructions to take Oscar with him *everywhere*?

Frustrating man.

But she would give him the benefit of the doubt. Perhaps he had a good reason for not bringing Oscar with him, although she couldn't think of a single one right off the top of her noggin. Shaking her head in dismay, she sniffed and guided Tugger along with her as she weaved her way across the room, smiling and greeting everyone she knew.

"Aaron," she called as she approached. He looked up and she waved at him. He jerked a nod in response. "I'm glad you could make it."

He audibly let out the breath he'd been holding. He was obviously not a people person the way Ruby was. She was outgoing and received her energy from being around other people, so it was hard for her to even vaguely understand what it would be like not to want to be at the center of attention—something Aaron was clearly loath to do. He looked as if he wanted to crawl into the nearest hole, if the earth would be so cooperative as to open one for him.

"I'm happy to see you," he said. "I was starting to worry maybe you weren't coming. You wouldn't desert me now, would you?"

She shook her head. "Oh, I never miss services. Nor do my brothers and sisters and my grandpa. We were christened right here in this church, and this is where we grew up and learned all about the Lord."

"And your parents?" he asked.

It had been over five years, but grief still had a way of smacking her sideways at the most inopportune of moments. She knew it showed in her expression.

"I'm sorry," he said, reaching out and pressing his palm to her shoulder. "I shouldn't have asked. It's none of my business."

"Maybe I can tell you about them later."

"Sure. Later," he agreed. "It's about time to head into the sanctuary, anyway. Cool dog, by the way." He gestured at Tugger. "I thought you said you didn't have any tough dogs in your program."

A laugh escaped Ruby's lips. "Oh, Aaron, if only you knew what you were saying. Tugger here is the *least* daunting dog we have in the program. He's a total sweetheart. But trust me when I say he's not quite the right dog for you. He's actually being trained for use in therapy work."

"You have your pit bull doing therapy work and a poodle with a marine handler? It seems to me you've got it backward."

She smiled and shook her head but didn't bother arguing. She'd spent her whole adult life training service dogs. It wasn't about how they looked on the outside. It was all about their temperaments. Speaking of poodles, however...

"Since you mentioned Oscar—where, exactly, is he right now?"

"Back at the B and B. Don't worry. I crated him just like you told me to do. I even gave him a toy. He's safe and happy right now."

"No. What I told you to do was take Oscar with you everywhere you go."

"Not church, though, surely. I wouldn't have even considered bringing him here."

Ruby raised an eyebrow and gestured her chin toward Tugger.

"*Especially* church," she countered. "Think about it, Aaron. Oscar has to learn to avoid distractions and stay quiet while he's working. He can't do that if you don't keep him with you. Besides, he's going to be your permanent service dog. From now on he'll be with you twenty-four hours out of every day. How else can he be there when you may need help? That could happen anywhere, even at church."

"Oh." He looked as if someone had let the wind out of his sails. But then his expression hardened—probably because she'd mentioned he might need help from time to time and was too stubborn to admit that was the case.

"It was an honest mistake," she said in a reassuring tone. He'd already reached out to her, so this time she was the one reaching for his arm. Her palm landed on his bicep, and his muscles contracted. Off went her mind, zinging around in la-la land instead of paying attention.

She reminded herself that Aaron was a bullheaded marine, her client, and so far, she'd had nothing but trouble with him.

And yet—*biceps*.

That was it. It was time to jump back into the dating pool. She was going to the next country dance, and she was going to dance every set with as many different single men as Whispering Pines could dole out, at least those who she hadn't had bad breakups with. Perhaps God would bless her and there'd be some new handsome, unattached men in town. Because she was treading on very thin ice when she started noticing her *client* as a very attractive man.

Especially Aaron.

He'd be here four weeks, and then he'd be gone.

This whole crazy situation probably belonged on a television drama. The association between her and Aaron would thankfully draw to a close at the end of training.

So why didn't that make her feel as relieved as it ought to have done?

Now, how was Aaron to know that he was supposed to bring Oscar to *church*, of all places? He'd read through all the documents Ruby had given him—several times over, in fact. It wasn't easy to absorb. There were so many details to memorize, everything from when and how to feed Oscar to what to expect from the dog when they went out for a walk together. He didn't know how he would ever remember everything.

He supposed that was what these four weeks of instruction were for. Training exercises. Just like in the marines, a man had to practice, practice and then practice some more, until everything became second nature to him. When he was in the middle of a firefight, even if he didn't remember everything he was supposed to do, his training would automatically snap in.

He supposed that applied to Oscar, as well. As a sergeant, he'd been in charge of training and leading the marines in his squad, and he knew it was a matter of repeating exercises over and over again until they were second nature and then debriefing the men thoroughly after each session.

This whole thing with Ruby and Oscar was different, and yet in many ways it was vaguely similar to his past experiences. Perhaps he ought to treat this new canine-training exercise the same way he'd conquered the rest of his life. He didn't like it, but then again, he didn't have to. It was only four weeks, after all, and then he could decide whether this was truly going to work out for him.

Worst-case scenario, he would walk away from it all in the end without a service dog, but since he wasn't yet entirely convinced that he needed one in the first place, what did it matter in the long run? It wasn't as if he'd raised his hand and volunteered to be here. He still had major doubts about this whole program, especially about his froufrou dog. Although, if he was being honest, he hadn't totally hated relaxing on the couch the night before watching ESPN with Oscar curled up next to him, and he could imagine doing it on a regular basis. Both of them had munched on beef jerky—a high-protein treat Oscar apparently enjoyed as much as Aaron.

But bringing a dog to church?

He just wouldn't have thought of it, and he certainly wouldn't have liked it. Talk about embarrassing. If he didn't already stand out like a sore thumb just by being here, Oscar would surely have drawn every eye. And yet he supposed what Ruby was saying made sense. The whole point of having Oscar was to help him when he needed it—which could theoretically mean church. It wasn't clear yet what Oscar was supposed to do that Aaron couldn't do himself.

And he most certainly wasn't quite at the point where he would be comfortable showing up for worship in a shirt and tie with a poufy poodle at his side. He wasn't sure if it was humility or humiliation poking at him, but he didn't like it either way.

In the foyer—where many church members were clustered in small groups, chatting and enjoying fellowship with one another—Ruby had quickly dragged him around to meet the rest of the Winslow crew. Like Ruby, they were an overtly friendly lot. Every one of Ruby's sisters had a dog at her heel, but no one other than Ruby, who'd made her private comments to him earlier, questioned why he hadn't brought Oscar with him on this outing or made him feel awkward or out of place.

But oh, did they ever rave on about how wonderful their sister was. As if he couldn't see it himself. Evidently, Ruby was both the brains and the heart behind A New Leash on Love. All her sisters worked in the program to one extent or another, but service dogs were Ruby's whole life's mission.

Shame washed over him as he heard story after story about Ruby's kind heart and all the time and effort she'd gone through to get to where she was today. And here he was, making things as difficult for her as he possibly could, from the moment he'd made his first pronouncement about not wanting to be here until right this moment, balking even now by not bringing Oscar with him today.

He followed the Winslows into the sanctuary, and Ruby gestured to the seat next to her on the pew. She really hadn't been kidding when she said her family took up two full pews. And yet Ruby purposefully made a spot for him so he wouldn't be alone during his first time worshipping at this new church. Even after everything he'd done to make things difficult for her, she was still being kind to him.

He was starting to feel wishy-washy about everything. Maybe he didn't really care for this mission, but when had that ever mattered in the past? He knew more than most that a marine did what he was ordered to do. Never mind that he was a vet and was here on the recommendation of his doctor as well as Major Kelley.

This operation hadn't played all the way through yet. He needed to man up and put his nose to the grindstone, really work the program and train as hard as he expected the marines under his supervision to do. Otherwise, how would he know for sure whether or not the program would work for others?

It wasn't even for his own sake that he needed to complete this mission. He might not like it, but many of his military brothers and sisters coming into the program after him would benefit from what Ruby could do for them even if he, Aaron, could not.

He wouldn't screw this up, no matter how much he wanted to drag his feet.

He tried to turn his attention to the worship but found his mind occasionally wandering to the pretty ginger-haired woman next to him. She was the complete opposite of the stereotypical fiery redhead. She conquered the world with soft words and a sweet voice. When she sang, it was an almost-physical sensation, her melodious soprano lifting the rafters in praise to the Lord.

He didn't sing. His voice was too low and raspy, and he couldn't carry a tune to save his life. And he wouldn't have opened his mouth even if he could. He didn't feel like singing.

He had a lot weighing down his heart that he wanted to share with God, so once the service had ended, he stayed behind to kneel and pray as everyone else left the sanctuary. He didn't even know Ruby had slipped into the pew behind him until he felt Tugger's wet nose snuffling the back of his neck.

Aaron stiffened as he whirled around in the pew.

Ruby was giggling behind her hand and looking at him apologetically.

He raised his brows.

"Now you know Tugger's secret gift," she whispered. "This is what he does. He's a lover puppy. There's nothing he likes better in this world than cuddling people, making sad *hoomans* happy again."

"Hmmph," he replied, fighting half a grin. "I get what you're trying to tell me. I think."

He definitely didn't want a *lover puppy* for his service dog, but Tugger would look a whole lot better than Oscar at the end of his leash any day of the week. He supposed there was a whole lot more to selecting a service dog than he'd realized.

"I don't mean to bother you if you're still praying. In truth, I was trying to wait quietly until you were finished so I could speak with you about something, but thanks to Tugger that didn't happen. I'll leave you to your prayers, and we'll talk another time."

"No, that's fine. I'm finished. What's up?"

The smile dropped from her lips, and he could tell she was fighting to find the right words. Her hands were curled over the back of the pew, and Aaron reached out and put one of his hands over hers. Her hand was shaking.

"You can talk to me," he assured her gently. Which was really a first in so many ways. He wasn't exactly the guy people came to with their problems.

"I know. Thank you. I—" She stopped, sounding as if she'd choked on the word. "Earlier you asked me about my parents. It's a story I think you should know. Bear with me, though. I still have a hard time talking about it."

He had to admit he was curious. He couldn't imagine how anything to do with her parents would relate to him in any way, but he remained silent and nodded for her to continue.

"My father was in the army. Infantry. I don't know what all he did there, but he was gone a lot. I know he was part of the Gulf War."

So, she wasn't as completely unfamiliar with the military lifestyle as he'd first believed her to be. She was an army brat. Was that why she was so desperate for this current contract—so she could help soldiers like her father?

"What happened to him?"

Her hands fisted tighter around the pew's edge, and she pinched her lips together. "He served his time and was honorably discharged at the end of it. Thankfully, he came home alive and without any external injuries."

She cringed when she realized what she'd said, but he simply scoffed and nodded for her to continue.

"But like many veterans, he wasn't the same man who'd left with stars in his eyes, believing he was going off to save the world. He might not have had any external injuries, no bullet holes or broken bones, but the internal scars were there and just as serious."

Aaron clenched his teeth. Without realizing it, he'd been stroking Tugger's head as they talked. The dog had simply wedged his body in close to him and leaned his weight on him, offering support in a way Aaron was only beginning to understand—what it was that made Tugger such a good therapy dog.

What he *did* understand was what Ruby's father had gone through. The scars, though invisible, were very real, as was the inexplicable draw to military life. Aaron had been one of those youngsters who, even before he'd finished high school, couldn't wait to sign his name on the dotted line. The recruiter who'd come to visit his school in an eye-catching blue uniform had told him he wouldn't be joining the marines—he'd *become* one.

He had become a marine, all right. The marines had changed his life, for better and for worse.

"Active military and our blessed veterans have saved the world numerous times over, and I cannot even begin to imagine what they have to go through every day. They—*you*—still face and beat the odds," said Ruby quietly, her eyes full of compassion. "I have so much respect for all of you. But for my father, it was too much."

Aaron narrowed his gaze on Ruby, his gut clenching as he realized where this conversation was leading. "In what way?"

"I don't know if it was the way he was internally wired or whether he just saw more than he was able to handle while on his tour of duty. He came home from the war with severe PTSD, possibly partially caused by a TBI. Like I said, he was honorably discharged, but after that, he could never hold a job down for more than a matter of months. He would start off determined to do well, but soon he'd be arriving late to work or not at all. After he'd been fired a few times, he just stopped trying altogether."

"I'm so sorry." His voice came out as thick as gravel.

"My mom was as much of a hero as he was. More, even. She refused to allow us to move from base to base. She was determined that we'd grow up here in Whispering Pines. She had six small children, yet she stepped up and took over running Winslow's Woodlands, which at the time was a much smaller ideation than what you see today, while my father ran off to war and came home a shell of a man, tinkering around in his shop and avoiding life."

Aaron understood her father better than Ruby ever would, but it wasn't something he'd talk about.

Not to Ruby. Not to anyone.

Internal scars, he understood.

The things he'd seen and experienced…

Her gaze caught his. She was begging for something, but he didn't know what.

"I'm so sorry," he said again. Then he realized she had only spoken of her mom and dad in the past tense and they weren't at church. "Your parents. They're…?"

"They died about five years ago, driving in the mountains on a dirt road with hairpin curves. Sometimes you can't see what's right around the corner because of the mountain paths. You're supposed to honk and wait for a response, but from what investigators said, my dad didn't do that. Or he didn't wait long enough if he did honk. He caused the accident that killed both him and my mom on impact and sent their SUV rolling down a steep mountainside. Thankfully, the other driver was only minimally injured."

"That's why you want this military contract," Aaron concluded for her. "To help men and women like your father so maybe they won't pull away from the world. You'll not only be saving them but their families."

"Like my father. And my high school boyfriend Daniel. He came back so angry—not the same boy I knew at all. He's in prison now."

And that, Aaron realized, was exactly the path he'd been on before coming to A New Leash on Love. Hiding from the world and wallowing in his pain, both internal and external.

Shutting down.

Sometimes letting his anger overwhelm him.

Tears cascaded down Ruby's face. She sniffled and dashed them away with the corner of her blouse, but her cheeks were still damp.

Aaron reached out and brushed her cheek with the pad of his thumb.

"Service dogs really do make a difference," she said, pulling herself back together. "I know they do. I've witnessed it with my own eyes enough times to believe that with all my heart. I've worked with many injured clients in the past, although you're my first marine."

"Don't hold that against the marines," he joked, trying to tease a smile from her.

It worked. One moment his heart was squeezing with the weight of her sorrow, and the next her radiant smile lifted both her countenance and his.

"I've said this before, but if you really try and work this program, Oscar may make all the difference in the world to you."

At the moment, *Ruby* was the one making the real difference in his life, but he wasn't about to say that out loud.

Instead, he pressed his lips together and nodded in agreement. "Yes, ma'am. One thing you ought to know about me—I may not agree with all my reasons for being here, but I'm a perfectionist. I'll follow the program to the letter. Not so much for me but for my military brothers and sisters who will be following me in this program when it becomes a success. I understand how important it is to get Major Kelley to sign off on this thing for the benefit of other veterans."

"I'll take it," she said, removing her hand from underneath his and standing, commanding Tugger to her side. "But Aaron?"

"What?"

"If you'd give Oscar half a chance, he'll work for you, too."

He didn't know that he'd ever completely believe that, but Ruby was so adamant, her light blue eyes sparkling with such warmth and confidence, that he couldn't help but agree, if only to make her feel better.

"I'm sure he will."

Chapter Four

Ruby wasn't at all sure what to do with Aaron. He was still the same grumpy marine with an attitude and a half who'd pulled up in her driveway the first day and who disagreed with practically everything she suggested, yet he was laser-focused on exactly what he needed to do to pass this program and help Ruby gain her military contract.

Not for himself, he often reminded her—as if she would forget what he'd said to her on that first day. He wasn't the one who needed help. This was all about those who would come after him who would actually find assistance using a service dog. Although Aaron was following the training she was offering him, that wasn't good enough for Ruby.

She wouldn't be happy until Aaron understood the benefits he was receiving from her program—until he admitted to her that Oscar was an essential and enduring part of his life and always would be.

She would keep working until Aaron truly believed in what she was doing here and acknowledged not only how it changed his life but also how it might help other veterans. And not just because Major Kelley said it must be so.

"I've been working with Oscar in our off-hours just like you taught me," he informed her, sounding as if the whole idea bored him. At the sound of his name, Oscar, who'd been sitting patiently at Aaron's heel, perked up. "Check this out."

He then put Oscar through a series of vocal commands, following each with a click from the clicker and at random times following his instructions with a treat. They'd started right out at the beginning with clicker training so the dog would know the exact moment he'd done what he'd been commanded.

Sit. Down. Stay. Heel.

And Oscar was already doing all of this off-leash. The pup appeared enamored of his new marine, but then again, how could he not be? Yes, Aaron needed a serious attitude check, but who wouldn't, after everything he'd been through?

Aaron released Oscar and he bounded away to run, stretch, bark, roll over and wiggle to scratch his back. Though Oscar was born to work, he also enjoyed break time when he could just be a dog. Ruby hoped Aaron appreciated those moments, as well, but she suspected it would take him some time to adjust to having a service *dog*—a friend and a playmate as well as a helper.

Ruby couldn't help but be impressed with how much progress he'd made with Oscar in just a few days. They'd been busy with paperwork and talking Aaron through the process of the entire program. In addition to what the military had given her in regard to Aaron, she'd needed to know what he expected out of the program, everything *he* wanted Oscar to perform for him and precisely where he felt the most physically vulnerable.

It hadn't been easy to get Aaron to open up and talk to her. She had the impression he didn't even know why he was here, other than that he was just following orders. She needed him invested in what he was doing and wasn't sure how to get there from here. It was a problem she hadn't ever run into before. All her previous clients had come to her eager for a service dog. Aaron was the total opposite.

They'd spent most of the day hashing out

the details so she could create a program that would best fit Aaron's needs. It was emotional trying to pry information out of Aaron, and it had worn both of them out. They'd finally finished in the middle of the afternoon and she'd let him off early, so she hadn't had time to have Aaron run Oscar through his paces, as important as that was.

She'd suspected Aaron wouldn't be forthcoming with his needs, which was why over the weekend she'd created a questionnaire specifically for Aaron. It was her little secret. She wasn't about to tell him he was the only one who would use this written questionnaire and that it wasn't her usual way of doing things. But she would do whatever she had to in order to discover what he needed out of the program without putting him on the spot. After he'd finished filling it out, they'd discussed his answers in detail. It had turned out to be a much easier process than verbally pressing him for answers, but it was still deeply emotional.

She had a feeling he was going to be surprised to discover how very much of a difference Oscar was going to make in his life. Every day, she intended to show him a little bit more until he was completely comfortable with his new service dog and couldn't imagine his life without Oscar.

"I'm impressed," she said after Aaron had finished running Oscar through his general obedience paces. "It's only been four days since I've seen you working with him, and it looks as if you've already got all the basics down. And off-leash, too. That's a wonderful start. I can tell you and Oscar have been busy. Are you ready for a little bit more of a challenge today?"

Aaron's chocolate-brown eyes lit up with interest and he grinned. "Now you're talking."

Why wasn't she surprised that Aaron would want to ramp things up a notch? As a marine, Ruby imagined Aaron's whole life had been about facing down challenges. Why stop now?

"Okay, then. Put Oscar's lead back on him and give me a minute. Let me grab a few of Oscar's friends, and we'll add some distractions to your workout."

She selected three well-trained dogs with whom Oscar was familiar as part of his pack and brought them, still on their leads, into the building next to Aaron. Oscar immediately responded to seeing his friends, his tail wagging so wildly it made his entire body quiver in excitement as he greeted the dogs. He definitely wanted to be let off the lead to play.

Aaron's brow furrowed and his grip tightened on Oscar's lead. "He's not going to go all uncontrollable on me, is he?"

"That's actually the point of this exercise. Oscar has to be able to stay focused on you no matter what distractions may come his way, including these dogs who are part of his pack. That's also the reason I insist you take him everywhere with you, up to and including church."

"And how do I get him to stay focused all the time? That sounds hard."

"First, *you* need to remain relaxed. As soon as you thought about Oscar running off on you, your shoulders tightened, as well as your grip on Oscar's lead. Oscar is going to pick up on it when you tense up as you just did. That'll only make him more likely to misbehave because he'll misread your signals and think you are in trouble. You used to command the men in your unit. I suspect this is similar. You've got to have a certain amount of trust in your dog that he'll make the right choices. That's where continued training will come in. For now, though, let's see what happens when we test him out. Call his name to get his attention and let him know it's time to work."

Aaron said Oscar's name, and despite the other dogs in the room, the poodle immediately moved to a heel position at Aaron's left side and sat, his full attention on him.

"Perfect," Ruby encouraged. "Just like you practiced, see? He knows what he's supposed to be doing. Now, let's see what happens when we release Tugger here as a distraction."

Ruby unleashed the exuberant brown-and-white pit bull without giving him any commands. Tugger was one of her most playful pups, which was the reason she'd selected him to throw a wrench into Oscar's training.

Tugger bounded off and ran around the perimeter of the training facility, his tail wagging and a big bully smile on his face as he sniffed every corner. When he'd checked out the entire area, he returned and play bowed to Oscar, his tail wagging a mile a minute.

"What's he doing?" Aaron asked, his brow lowering.

"It's called a *play bow*. He's enticing Oscar and encouraging him to join him for a puppy romp. But Oscar is better trained than that, and you have him under your command right now. Until you release him, he shouldn't move out of position. Try to relax your shoulders more so he doesn't pick up on your anxiety."

"It's not anxiety," Aaron snapped back.

Clearly not.

Ruby bit back her amusement and refrained from rolling her eyes, knowing it would only put Aaron in more of a snit. He was so far out of his comfort zone it wasn't even funny, but he would never admit it in a thousand years, so there was no reason to point it out to him.

And they were only at the beginning of their training. It was going to be a long four weeks. Aaron was definitely Ruby's biggest challenge to date, bar none.

"Here comes Dandy," she said in an enthusiastic tone, unleashing the black Labrador retriever. Dandy joined Tugger, bolting across the room at full speed. They play wrestled with each other and barked up a storm.

Oscar was clearly interested in what was going on around him with the loose dogs. His tail was still wagging, but his hind side was firmly on the floor, and he hadn't moved an inch, despite his clear desire to do so. Instead, he looked up at Aaron, awaiting his next word.

"Give him the *down* command," Ruby said. "That'll bring his focus completely back to you."

Aaron's jaw tightened but he followed her instructions. "Oscar, down."

Oscar immediately flopped down next to his heel, and he used the clicker to let the poodle know the moment he'd done as he'd been told.

"Wonderful," Ruby praised, half to the dog and half to the rugged marine. "I have to say again how proud I am of the two of you. I can really tell you have been hard at work during your off-time."

"Isn't that the whole point?" Aaron asked with a wry half smile.

"Indeed, it is. It's just that I don't usually see such fine progress so quickly. Well done, Aaron."

"It's not all on me. You already had Oscar trained before I ever showed up here. You did the hard work. Oscar just has to get used to me and my way of commanding."

And for you to understand your service dog, Ruby silently added.

Ruby couldn't imagine how many hours Aaron had put in with the poodle, but Oscar had clearly already bonded with Aaron. Yet Aaron was still looking at Oscar as a mountain he had to climb, a mission he had to accomplish. There wasn't yet any personal connection between them, and that was the key to a successful relationship between a human and a service dog.

But maybe that was it. Ruby was really good at training dogs, but this time it wasn't about the dog. It was about the human.

She wasn't speaking Aaron's language. If she approached the whole dog-training thing as if she were giving Aaron a mission, he might better understand what she was attempting to do.

Except the thought of ordering Aaron to do anything was intimidating, to say the least. His insides were as tough as his outside appeared. There wasn't any softness in US Marine Sergeant Aaron Jamison.

Mission impossible.

Aaron walked Oscar down the main street in town, Lone Elk Avenue, partially to continue the training from earlier in the day with the street full of distractions in the form of people, cars and a variety of sounds, but also so he could get to know Whispering Pines a little bit better. It made him nervous to be out here, but he forced himself to greet those he'd met at church and ignored any curious stares that were shot his direction.

He didn't usually spend much time in public. He hated that people might stare at him, whether out of curiosity or because of his disability, and he was afraid Oscar might pick up on his nerves. But he knew he needed to practice, and what better way than in a situation in which he was uncomfortable?

He spent all his free time with Oscar, going over what they'd learned so far in training to prove to himself that he hadn't completely lost his edge, and yet hawk-eyed Ruby had no qualms about pointing out every mistake he made, every error, no matter how small. The last time he'd been under this kind of microscope had been at Parris Island marine corps basic training. And he'd felt far more self-confident there than he did now.

He'd been a whole man back then.

Ruby didn't bark out commands like a drill sergeant. Just the opposite, in fact. She was soft-spoken and smiled a lot, and her corrections were firm but gentle. She used positive reinforcement rather than putting him down. He wasn't used to seeing happy faces, especially pretty female ones, and her smiles made his nerves crackle and his skin itch. Oscar might be easily distracted by his doggy friends, but *Ruby* was Aaron's real distraction, and he knew he needed to work through it just as he was working Oscar through his.

The only change was the scenery—from a

dry stark brown desert to the scent of pine and green everywhere. He'd gone from spending his time with big brutes as cold and tough as he was to hanging out with, of all things, a froufrou dog and a beautiful woman.

Even though Ruby had given him a notebook full of instructions, it was a lot to remember, and he'd quickly learned if he hesitated, he would lose Oscar's attention. That's why the clicker was so important—so the poodle would immediately know when he'd done the right thing.

It had been a long day, and his stomach was growling for some dinner. At first, he'd intended to go back to the bed-and-breakfast where he was staying. They didn't typically serve dinner there, but they had a well-stocked community refrigerator. He'd purchased deli meat and sandwich fixings when he'd first arrived, but his nose had just picked up the smell of fresh pizza, and he was salivating in earnest.

"Do you smell that pizza, boy?" he asked Oscar, then felt his face rapidly heating along with the beat of his heart.

He let his nose guide him down the street past a hair salon and a store that sold souvenirs both for Colorado in general and Whispering Pines in particular. He spent a moment window-shopping and made a mental note to return and purchase a Whispering Pines hoodie before he left.

Finally, he found the pizza joint from which all those wonderful smells were emanating.

Sally's Pizza.

The place was packed, which he supposed made sense, as it was a Friday evening. When he glanced in the window, he realized there wasn't a free table anywhere. The food clearly tasted as good as it smelled.

No matter. He'd just grab a pizza with everything except anchovies to go and relax back at the B and B.

And then he remembered he had Oscar by his side. Church was bad enough, but a restaurant? There were no signs specifically banning dogs from entering, but at the same time, he was fairly certain there must be state or federal laws against such things. Wouldn't the health department pitch a fit if he were to walk in with his dog?

He sighed internally. No pizza for him, then.

Bummer. He'd really been looking forward to it.

Suddenly, a black truck with a dual cab pulled up next to the curb, parallel parking in front of the pizza restaurant even as the electric window on the passenger side came sliding down.

To his surprise, it was Ruby—and Tugger, who immediately popped his head out the window and barked a happy hello at Oscar.

"I see you had the same idea as me," Ruby said with a chuckle. "You're probably at least as hungry as I am after all the work we did today. I guarantee you that Sally's pizza is the best you'll ever taste. And tonight is open mic night, so you're in for an extra treat. My brother Frost brought his guitar."

Before he could say a word, Ruby had hopped out of the truck and come around to the passenger side, opening the door and letting Tugger out. He was dressed in a bright red service-dog vest, and Ruby quickly snapped a lead on him.

"Aren't you going to roll up your window and lock the door?" he asked, surprised when she appeared to be ignoring it.

She glanced back at her truck, which couldn't be more than a year or two old. "Hmm? Oh...no. No need. That's not really a thing in Whispering Pines. I'll only be inside the restaurant for an hour or so, and anyway, my friends and neighbors watch out for each other."

"You're kidding me, right?"

"Nope. There are definite advantages to living in a small town, and safety is at the top of the list."

He shook his head and let out a low whistle. "I guess."

"Ready?" she asked him with a smile as Tugger immediately moved to her left heel, his attention now completely focused on her.

Aaron's attention was likewise fixated on the beautiful woman with the pit bull.

Then her question penetrated his thick skull. Aaron shook his head. "I've got Oscar with me. Pizza sounds great, but I didn't plan ahead. Do you want to hold him while I go in and order for both of us?"

He might be behind the times, but he still believed in the guy paying, even if this wasn't technically a date. But when she didn't immediately respond, he continued.

"Or I could hold Tugger for you, and you could do the ordering."

She grinned. "You're supposed to have Oscar with you, remember? All the time, including restaurants. I have a better idea. There's a table in the corner that was just vacated. How about you take Oscar and save us the spot, and I'll do the ordering?"

"With Tugger?"

"Of course."

"And Sally—if there is actually a Sally who owns this joint—doesn't mind that we're bringing in dogs?"

"Mind? Sally Jensen is a regular donor to our service-dog program, and she's never met a pup she didn't love. Customers, either. She's super friendly and I can't wait for you to meet her."

Again, Aaron shook his head. This whole experience was so unlike anything he'd ever known before. He was about to meet the *Sally* in Sally's Pizza? That wouldn't have ever happened in Kansas City, where he was originally from. "Sally" would have been a major franchise with an owner named Bob. But despite his doubts, he opened the door and allowed Ruby and Tugger to go in ahead of him.

"I'll order at the counter and then join you at our table. What's your poison?" Ruby asked. "I like the one with veggies piled on."

"The everything-but-the-kitchen-sink kind," Aaron said, surprised that he was actually starting to relax. Ruby's smile did that to him. "Everything, that is, except anchovies. Not much of a little-fish guy."

"You got it," she said. "No fishies. Now, hurry before we lose our table."

"Yes, ma'am."

"'Ma'am'? Seriously, Aaron?" She wrinkled her nose at him.

He offered her an apologetic smile and turned toward the booth in the corner. There was a small platform against one wall rigged with a microphone and stool, and a young lady was singing a country song. Aaron felt awkward weaving his way through the tables to the vacated one, yet no one appeared to notice Oscar at all. *He* got a few curious looks, but only, he suspected, because he was a stranger to town and not necessarily because he'd brought a dog into the restaurant with him. Most customers were politely watching the young lady at the microphone.

He was feeling self-conscious when he knew he didn't need to be. It was just that he always felt as if people were staring at him.

Minutes later, Ruby joined him at the table. "Sally's on her way out to meet you. She's a bit over-the-top," she warned. "But I've never met a kinder woman."

Sally chose that moment to arrive at their table, bearing water glasses and an enormous welcoming smile.

"I have to admit I was hoping you'd be wearing your uniform," she told Aaron, swatting her hand his direction. "I've always had a thing for men in uniforms," Sally teased with a cheeky laugh.

Heat flooded Aaron's face. Sally was old enough to be his grandmother, and she was flirting with him like a teenager.

"I'm Sally Jensen. And you must be US Marine Corps Sergeant Aaron Jamison."

"Yes, ma'am," he said. "But please just call me Aaron." Sally beamed. "I have to say I'm surprised there's even a real person named Sally at Sally's Pizza, and not only that, but you've come out to personally introduce yourself even though your restaurant is bursting over with customers. I'm not used to it, but I appreciate the small-town touch."

"You'll find all of Whispering Pines opening their hearts to you," Sally assured him. "Good people, they are. I have to get back to the kitchen, but you just holler if you need anything."

"Sally Jensen of Sally's Pizza," Aaron murmured under his breath as he watched Sally walk away.

"I suppose she could have named it Fred's Pizza, but it wouldn't have quite the same ring to it, don't you think?"

"I feel as if I've been out of the loop for a very long time, and not just because I had more than one tour in Afghanistan."

"You haven't even tasted your pizza yet. You're about to be completely floored by the best pie ever."

"Speaking of," Sally said, returning to the table with two steaming pizzas heavily layered with extra cheese. "You two enjoy yourselves now." She ended by sending Aaron a saucy wink and a nod toward Ruby. The woman's words and actions suggested what was happening here at the table between Aaron and Ruby was a great deal more than them having accidentally met each other in front of the restaurant and deciding to share a meal together.

He met Ruby's gaze, wondering if she'd picked up on the same vibe. She raised her eyebrows so they nearly disappeared underneath her ginger bangs, but amusement glittered in her eyes. She knew exactly what Sally had been suggesting, and it didn't appear to bother her.

"I did warn you," she said. "No worries, though. She's just teasing. It's more on me than you. I've known her since I was a little girl. She's been pressuring me to have a serious relationship for some time now. Henpecking like everyone's grandmother who wants to see grandkids."

"And have you?" he asked, his curiosity spiking.

"Given Sally any honorary grandchildren? No," she said, purposefully misunderstanding his question.

He laughed.

Laughed.

How long had it been since that had happened?

"Had any serious relationships?" he clarified. Now he *had* to know the answer.

The pretty pink blush on her face clashed with her hair, and he wished he would have kept his mouth shut. It wasn't like him to blurt out personal questions. But at least if she was talking about herself, then she wasn't talking about him.

"Ruby."

Appearing startled, Ruby jumped to her feet at the sound of a man's deep voice.

"Daniel." She held a hand to her throat as she faced the tall, clean-shaven blond. "I thought you were… When did you…?"

Daniel's eyebrows knit together, and his Adam's apple bobbed when he swallowed. Aaron could sense the almost palpable tension between them. The name sounded familiar, but it took Aaron a few seconds to place it.

Ruby's high school boyfriend. The one who'd been in the army who had come back troubled. She hadn't said much about him, other than he'd…gone to prison?

"I'm out," Daniel confirmed, his tone hard.

"I'm glad to see that you're home again," Ruby told him. Aaron could hear the quiver in her voice and wondered if Daniel could hear it, as well. He didn't know how long the two of them had been together or if their breakup had to do with him going to prison or something else.

"Are you?" Daniel asked with a pointed look toward Aaron. Daniel's voice held the same underlying intensity Aaron had heard in too many veterans.

"Oh," Ruby said, sounding as if someone had punched her in the solar plexus. "Daniel, this is Aaron. Sergeant Aaron Jamison. He's a marine."

Daniel pressed his lips together and narrowed his eyes on Aaron.

Aaron held his hand out and waited. Daniel stared at it for a moment before reaching out to shake his hand.

"Nice to meet you," Aaron said, trying to put Daniel at ease.

Daniel cleared his throat before answering, "Same."

Aaron saw a flash of sadness in his eyes before his expression hardened.

Internally, Aaron vacillated between the yearning to protect Ruby's heart from what she must certainly be feeling right now and knowing just how difficult this must be for Daniel to come back to town only to find Ruby with another man—and a military man, no less. But though Daniel was clearly tense, he didn't sense anger coming from the man.

Oscar leaned against Aaron's calf, and Aaron reached down to stroke his head.

"I'm one of Ruby's clients," he said, trying to defuse the situation. "Oscar here is my service dog."

"Have a seat," Ruby offered, gesturing to the bench where she'd been sitting. "I was just introducing Aaron to Sally's wonderful pizza. Have you ordered yet? We can catch up while we eat."

Daniel shook his head. "I'm getting carry-out. My folks are expecting me."

"Oh. Of course, they'll be wanting to spend some time with you. Tell them hello for me," Ruby said.

"I will. And I'll see you at church on Sunday."

"Church?" Ruby parroted, sounding surprised.

Daniel smiled, but Aaron could see the sadness in his eyes again. "Some things changed when I was in prison."

"For the good," Ruby offered, reaching out to touch Daniel's arm.

Daniel scoffed and nodded. He glanced over at Aaron and then back at Ruby before continuing. "I know an apology isn't enough," he said.

"Daniel, I don't…"

"I need to say it. I'm sorry for the way things went down. I don't expect you to forgive me."

"I already have," Ruby said softly.

Daniel touched Ruby's shoulder, then turned and shook Aaron's hand before leaving to pick up his order at the counter.

Ruby sighed audibly as she slid back into the booth. Sadness poured from her gaze, and Aaron reached across the table for her hand.

"You okay?" He was in the middle of this situation whether he wanted to be or not, and he couldn't just sit there and watch Ruby suffer without saying anything.

Ruby paused before speaking. "I will be."

He waited to see if she wanted to talk about it but wasn't surprised when she pulled her hand from his and took a bite of her pizza.

"Mmm. Don't let your pizza get cold." And then, "Hey, look. Frost is playing."

Aaron's heart hurt, but not nearly as much as he expected hers did. He wished he could find something to say that would help her, but he wasn't any good at this kind of thing. Instead, he simply reached for his pizza and filled the large, empty gap of space with food.

Chapter Five

"What's on the agenda for today?" Aaron asked as he and Oscar entered into the agility dog run, where Ruby was jogging Dandy the black Labrador through some of the course obstacles. Dandy was a whiz weaving through the poles and zooming through the tunnels, so fast he was almost a blur and so excited that he couldn't stop barking.

She'd picked the Lab on purpose because he was so energetic. Seeing Daniel again had been a shock to her system, and she was trying to run off her own excess energy. She'd known he would eventually return to Whispering Pines but hadn't known when, mainly because she hadn't asked. After their bad breakup, the relationship between her and Daniel's parents was strained.

It sounded as if Daniel had found faith in prison. She hoped for his sake that was true.

Out of breath, Ruby called Dandy to her side and turned her attention to Aaron. Had he actually sounded enthusiastic about today's work?

It was now Tuesday of the second full week of training, and Ruby couldn't be happier about the progress Aaron and Oscar had made. It was clear they were working after hours, because Oscar was already bonding to him and, even more surprisingly, he to Oscar, even if he didn't realize it—or more to the point, wouldn't yet admit it.

He was doing incredibly well, but Ruby wasn't sure he'd want the praise she desired to heap upon him. She was used to reading the dogs' minds but was totally at a loss when it came to peering into the relentless marine's mind. As usual, he had a serious expression on his face, and his brows were low in concentration. Whenever she used to make such an expression when she was young, her mother would always tell her she'd better watch it, or her face would freeze that way.

Somehow, she didn't think Aaron would appreciate the joke.

Maybe that's what had happened to him after experiencing war. Had he been a different man earlier in his life the way Daniel had been? She'd been thrown by seeing Daniel again the previous Friday and how he still carried so much anger in his heart. She'd been glad Aaron had been with her.

She honestly didn't think Aaron was anything like Daniel, though he may have become worse after his accident. He didn't constantly fume the way her father had done, and Daniel still did. After spending some time with Aaron, she suspected his heart was now made of ice, which mirrored itself in his expression.

"Can Oscar and I have a go at this course?" he asked, his eyes lighting with interest as he perused the obstacles. "I'll bet he can rock this thing."

"We'll eventually get to that, and yes, I have no doubt you and Oscar will have a blast. But I have something else exciting planned for today," she told him, hoping he couldn't see her cringe before she'd even told him what was on the day's agenda.

She'd planned a mountain hike to start working on forward momentum, where Oscar would lend him strength when his own body failed him—and she intended to push him to that point. Whether he was willing to admit it or not, she knew that such a hike, even on a relatively easy trail, would be physically taxing on his body. Today wouldn't be a good day for him to try the agility course. Not until she had a better idea of how his stamina would hold out.

Disappointment crossed his face, and she hesitated, wondering if she should change her plans. But in the long run, she knew the only way to really test his stamina was to force him to push through difficult things.

Still, a couple of agility obstacles couldn't hurt.

"I suppose one or two obstacles wouldn't hurt," she said, unable to resist the pressure of her heart. "Walk Oscar over to the A-frame and remove his leash."

He pumped his fist in triumph, and Ruby's heart beat double time. She couldn't help but smile as he half walked, half jogged Oscar over to the yellow-and-blue-painted obstacle. He appeared slightly wobbly to Ruby's hawk eyes, and she wondered if he was completely aware of his imbalance or whether he'd shoved that knowledge aside the way he likely did his internal scars.

If he wasn't ready to face the truth about his external injuries, he certainly would be by the end of today.

But he had to face the truth about himself. That was why she was here and what she

did—on purpose, so he would finally understand how important his service dog and her
program were.

"His paws have to touch the yellow-painted
surface on the bottom of each side of the
A-frame," she explained. "Just command him
to *hup* and gesture toward the A-frame. He'll
take it from there."

"And...*hup*!" Aaron exclaimed, swinging his arm wide and looking like a kid in a
candy store, he was so excited.

Again, Ruby noticed a waver in his balance, but again, she remained silent about it.
With most clients she'd be pointing out the
obvious, but with Aaron she suspected her
observation would have the completely opposite effect of what she wanted. He'd realize it himself before long.

Oscar bolted for the A-frame at a full run
and was up and down within seconds, spring-
ing off the back side halfway down. His paws
didn't come remotely close to touching the
yellow paint at the bottom.

"He didn't do it right," Aaron said, frowning. "He was supposed to touch the yellow
paint, but he jumped too soon. How do I fix
that?"

Men.

Instead of reveling in the excitement of the

moment and what he had accomplished with Oscar, he only saw the flaws in the execution and wanted to *fix things*. With everything she'd observed so far, he was equally as critical of himself.

"Oscar is just overexcited. This time snap his leash back on and walk with him through the obstacle. That will force him to move slowly at whatever pace you set for him," she explained. She brought Dandy over and demonstrated what she wanted to see Aaron and Oscar do. "Oscar is just in a frenzy because he gets to share this moment with you. Don't worry. He'll settle down and get better with practice."

Aaron followed Ruby's lead and took Oscar over the A-frame at a slow walk, the dog's paws successfully tromping over the yellow paint on both sides this time. Aaron squared his shoulders, but Ruby couldn't see any other outward signs of the triumph he must be feeling. He approached everything as a mission, after all, and slow going as it was, this little obstacle was mission accomplished.

"What else do we get to do? You said two obstacles," he reminded her.

"I did," she agreed with a smile, surprised that he wanted to continue after the first fail. "What looks good to you?"

"The whole thing. But I know we're not ready for some of the obstacles yet."

"Oscar is especially talented at jumping. Do you want to try sending him through that hoop over there?" She pointed in the direction of the obstacle, a vertical circle through which Oscar would leap.

"Awesome," he said, walking Oscar toward the obstacle. "It looks just like a circus trick. How do I get him to do this one?"

"Same idea as before. Gesture and tell him *hup*. He knows what to do."

"Oscar, *hup*," Aaron urged, swinging his arm toward the circle.

This time, Oscar didn't take a run at the obstacle, as many dogs would have had to do to get the height he needed. Two steps and then he stretched and effortlessly flew through the hoop, gracefully landing on the other side without so much as a single hair touching the equipment.

"Wow," Aaron said, crouching beside his dog and giving him not one, but two pieces of liver treat. "Good boy, Oscar. That was incredible."

Ruby beamed with gratitude. For once, Aaron wasn't complaining about his froufrou dog. He actually looked thrilled.

"Are you ready for a real challenge today?

Something even bigger than the agility course?" She decided she'd frame today's encounter in as positive a light as possible.

"Always." He stood up and met her gaze. "Whatcha got for me?"

"I thought it would be fun and relaxing for us to take a little hike into the Rocky Mountains. We've got many lovely trails in the area that are absolutely beautiful—lofty trees, colorful wildflowers, babbling streams. Some of my favorite trailheads even start right here next to Winslow's Woodlands."

In truth, Ruby knew perfectly well it wasn't going to be a *relaxing* day, especially with a marine who expected so much out of himself physically. Aaron didn't know it yet, but hiking was going to require all the new skills he'd been learning with Oscar and then some. But Ruby didn't want to start out on a sour note, so she didn't mention that part.

She slipped on a backpack filled with water, snacks, medical supplies and typical hiking paraphernalia and adjusted the straps to fit her small frame.

"Where's mine?" he asked, frowning again. Always frowning about something. Sometimes Ruby wanted to take him by his broad shoulders and shake him just to get a smile out of him.

"Your…?"

"Backpack."

She raised her brows. "Oh, we don't need two. This is a relatively simple half-day hike, and I've got everything we need in this one pack. I want you to focus on working with Oscar unencumbered. You'll be doing a lot of new things today."

His expression hardened, and there he was again, the tough, stubborn marine with whom Ruby would just as soon not have to deal.

"Look, Ruby, I've spent the last however many years of my life toting backpacks way heavier than whatever you've got in there. I used to wear one everywhere, even in the hottest climates. Everything I did, I did with seventy-five pounds of gear on my back. I promise you I can take it."

Ruby sighed. "It's not about taking it, Aaron. And I have no doubt you're perfectly capable of carrying a backpack no matter how heavy it is."

A heavy backpack was exactly what he *didn't* need right now with his balance problems. Why wouldn't he just admit to the truth?

Probably because he hadn't yet *accepted* the truth. And somehow, within the next three weeks, Ruby was going to have to get Aaron over that mountain, which was much higher than the one they'd be facing today.

Ruby sighed. "It's just not necessary right now. Don't fight me on this. I need you to fully concentrate on working with Oscar."

"I'm not moving one inch until I have that pack on my back," he insisted, locking his gaze with hers. His brown eyes were almost black, matching his mood.

Stubborn man!

She paused, trying to think of another way to talk him out of it, but in the end, she couldn't think of any other reason for her to keep the backpack than those she'd already mentioned. Clearly, she hadn't convinced him.

And she supposed he was right. As a marine in Afghanistan, he would have been toting a much heavier pack around as he completed his missions. This little thing couldn't weigh more than fifteen pounds and was nothing compared to that.

She loosened the shoulder straps and dropped the pack to the earth.

"Fine. You want it so bad, it's yours." Frustration seethed from her tone, but he didn't appear to notice.

He jerked his chin in a brief nod and picked up the pack, quickly adjusting the shoulder straps to match his much larger frame. "Good. Now, point the way to the trailhead and let's be off."

A few minutes later, they were hiking along a trail barely wide enough to fit two people side by side along with their dogs. Ruby had purposefully selected this intermediate trail because it had some incline, which was important to the lesson she intended to teach today. She also liked it because of known obstacles—tree roots, small streams to ford, loose stones and the occasional fallen tree over which to crawl.

It was agility for humans—or perhaps vaguely similar to a marine boot camp obstacle course—and it was physical therapy for Aaron. Despite his balance issues, he shot ahead with his long strides and then turned around to face her, grinning, his breath coming in quick gasps and sweat beading on his forehead.

It was nice to see him smile. She'd suspected he would enjoy being out in nature, but he looked like a different man. His scruffy face appeared fresh, and his eyes glowed with pleasure. A cluster of butterflies burst from her stomach, and she had to swallow hard to push back the emotions flooding her.

The fresh air and enjoying God's creation

were working as she'd hoped they would, but Ruby knew the most difficult part of the hike was yet to come.

Before they finished for the day, Aaron would have to make use of Oscar whether he wanted to or not, and she wasn't at all sure how that was going to go.

This was more like it—treading down a dirt path carved into majestic Colorado mountains and breathing in the sights and sounds. It was impossible *not* to believe in God when he viewed meadows of colorful wildflowers and burbling streams, heard birdsong and watched a red-tailed hawk soaring in the breeze.

They stopped to admire a hidden waterfall they'd found, and Ruby pulled well-stacked hoagie sandwiches out of the backpack.

"I always get hungry when I hike," she said, passing him a sandwich and a bottle of water. "Something about the fresh air, I think. I feel as if I could walk on forever when I'm out here on the trails."

"Me, too," he agreed, biting into his sandwich. He was worried, however, that what he'd agreed to wasn't completely true. While he was definitely enjoying the scenery and the mountain hike, he was starting to feel it in his limbs and lungs. He had to consciously think about his balance in order to stay upright and not drag his left leg.

Anger flooded through him, and he turned to look out at the waterfall so Ruby wouldn't see his expression. It wasn't her fault he was half a man who couldn't even handle a simple day hike. What had the war turned him into?

A weakling?

No way was he going to let Ruby know how he was feeling. She was so full of joy she looked as if she were about to lift off and fly through the rest of the hike like that hawk soaring above them. Her enthusiastic smile was contagious, and he tried to grasp on to that feeling.

He'd been trained to *make it* without showing emotion. He'd done it before and he would do so now, no matter what it took on his end. It was all about self-discipline. She'd given him a gift today. The cool breeze and fresh mountain air were so much better than any of the long, tortuous marches in baking heat he'd endured in the past.

He could *do* this.

But when they finished their sandwiches and started hiking again, they turned a corner, and he was suddenly faced with a fairly steep incline—one he wasn't certain he could conquer. Oh, he'd vanquished much tougher situations, but that was before his accident, and he hadn't been with Ruby then.

What if he couldn't handle the incline? He'd be humiliated beyond measure if his lack of balance sent him woozily to the ground or if he had to back off because the trail was too steep.

He pressed his fingers to his eyes, concentrating. As he'd learned in boot camp, beating whatever obstacles that were in front of him was as much or more about his mind as it was his body. He needed to pull himself together and conquer this mountain.

"Okay," he said. "Let's do this."

"It looks steep, right?" Ruby asked, pressing one fist to the small of her back and making no move to start up the mountain.

"Yes, ma'am." He refused to say more than that, afraid he would give himself away if he kept speaking.

"It is. And I brought you here on purpose. This is where Oscar is going to step in and make your life easier."

Oscar?

"And how's he going to do that, exactly?" he muttered as heat filled his face. As if a dog was going to help him climb this mountain. What was Oscar going to do, drag him forward? He was going to be so glad when these four weeks were over and he could go hide out in his small apartment in the suburbs of Kansas City. If he could give Oscar back to Ruby without messing up her opportunity for the military contract and hurting Ruby's feelings, he would. He really didn't need the poodle, though he knew Ruby would never agree.

"He'll lend you extra forward motion and help you with your balance."

Ruby paused and he gritted his teeth and waited for her to continue.

"Aaron?"

"What?" He realized only after he'd spoken that he'd barked back at her. "Sorry," he muttered under his breath, but he doubted Ruby could hear him.

"If I can feel your anxiety, Oscar definitely can."

"I'm not anxious."

"I can clearly see you're a big ball of nerves right now. Your muscles are so tight I doubt you would be able to turn your head. You can either keep telling yourself you're not anxious or we can conquer this mountain together."

Together.

How she put up with his nonsense was beyond him. There was a good reason he was a loner. Most people would have written him off, if not the day she'd met him then definitely now, with the kind of attitude he'd displayed in the last ten minutes.

But not Ruby.

She was willing to keep reaching out her hand to the dog who bit her—and he wasn't talking about any of the service dogs in her program.

"Okay," he finally agreed. "How, exactly, is Oscar supposed to help me?"

"It's going to be easier for you to experience what I'm talking about than for me to try to explain what I mean. Grab the handle of his vest and start hiking up the hill. Don't worry about how fast you're going. Oscar will adjust to your stride."

"Fine." He slipped his fist into the handle on Oscar's leather vest and strode as fast as he could up the mountain at about the pace he'd done when he was in marine training.

It only took a couple of minutes for him to discover what Ruby was talking about. He hated to admit it, but Oscar was helping him with continued forward momentum, and there were a couple of times he was glad the poodle was with him when his balance went wonky. He probably would have fallen down had Oscar not been there.

"What do you think?" she asked when they stopped for a break.

At first, he considered pretending he didn't understand what she was asking, but he knew perfectly well her beautiful blue eyes had missed nothing. She'd seen him pause. She'd probably seen the times he'd leaned on Oscar to regain his balance and for support on more than one occasion. She'd heard his breathing increase along with the incline. She'd no doubt watched him stumble and nearly fall if it weren't for the dog by his side bolstering him up.

"I have to admit Oscar is useful on a hike," he finally said, clenching his jaw as humiliation washed over him.

"That's it? That's all I get?"

"Yep." If she was expecting a long, drawn-out monologue on the benefits of a service dog, she was waiting on the wrong guy.

He didn't want to talk about it.

Nor did he want to think about what he'd become, that he needed a dog for a simple mountain hike.

She studied him for a minute before a radiant smile graced her face. "Okay. I'll take it."

And then she hiked off ahead of him without another word.

Chapter Six

It was Saturday, and Ruby's weekend was full, as it always was. She tended to ignore household chores during the week while she was training her dogs and their new handlers. Then she'd make up for it on Saturday. Sunday was busy with church and spending time with her family.

She and several of her siblings still lived in the large Winslow cabin so they could split duties in caring for her grandfather. Today it was her turn to tidy up the house—sweep and mop the hardwood floors, dust the furniture and give the kitchen a good, thorough cleaning. Everyone was responsible for cleaning their own bathrooms. Since both Winslow's Woodlands and A New Leash on Love were located on the Winslows' properties, there were still four adult children living at home—

Ruby, both her brothers Sharpe and Frost, and her sister Felicity—along with their aging grandfather, whom they all took care of. This may have appeared odd to some, but they'd always been a close family, and for right now, at least, it worked for them.

Her other two sisters, Molly and Avery, had flown the nest when they'd married, each pursuing their own dreams with their new life partners and their families. Ruby now had two nephews and one niece whom she fiercely loved. After Daniel had come home so troubled and their relationship had fallen apart, she'd been more than a little gun-shy when it came to trust issues. Ruby had always assumed she'd find her person and leave the nest at some point, but it wasn't as if a line of potentially perfect life partners were queuing on her doorstep.

Not that she believed in long lines of prospectives, anyway. She was one of those hopeless romantics who believed in one true love, a man she would immediately recognize as God's gift to her—which was probably why she was going to end up a lonely old spinster, an elderly cat lady—although at present she didn't have any cats.

Elderly dog lady?

That could happen.

She chuckled at the thought as she swept and mopped the hardwood floor in the family room, singing and dancing like Snow White as she worked. She was way too busy trying to figure out how she was going to get one particularly stubborn marine to the finish line to worry about romance. Love would have to stay on the back burner for now.

Even though Aaron was clearly trying harder to succeed in the challenges with which she presented him, he still balked at having to use Oscar the poodle, especially on those days when she brought Tugger along. How many times could the man complain about a froufrou dog before it became nothing more than an annoyance?

Get over it already.

And that was nothing to say of his utter unwillingness to admit to his weaknesses. Most of her clients started there so they could immediately move forward rather than being stuck at the starting line. They didn't depend on Ruby to prove anything to them but were perfectly aware of why they'd sought her help in the first place. They were looking for the assistance Ruby knew she, her dogs and her program could provide.

And then there was Aaron...

She sighed. This was the weekend—her

two days off to catch up with her chores and possibly find a little time to relax. So why couldn't she get Aaron off her mind?

She finished mopping and scrubbed the kitchen counters with extra vigor until everything shined, but she still felt restless. Maybe relaxing out on the back porch with a cup of coffee and a good book would help.

Or not.

After reading the same paragraph over and over for fifteen minutes, she scoffed and shook her head, slamming the book closed.

There was no getting out of it. She was going to have to go over to the bed-and-breakfast and put herself out of her misery—since Aaron was the direct cause of her misery.

As if that made any sense.

Deciding to walk to negate some of the energy charging through her, she put a vest and lead on Tugger, who enjoyed hiking almost as much as he enjoyed loving on people. It was a mild, cloudy day for August, and she relished the fresh air and exercise.

When she reached the B and B, she thumped up the stairs two at a time. Avery's gregarious Texan husband, Jake Cutter, opened the door for her before she could even so much as reach out a hand to knock. In his free arm, he held nine-month-old baby Felix, who pumped his arms and legs in excitement and babbled cheerfully at Ruby.

"Well, hey there, Ruby. Nice day for a walk," Jake said in his Texas accent and offered her a toothy grin.

"Hi, Jake. Hey, Felix, you chubby-cheeked sweetheart," she said, reaching out a finger for the baby to clasp. He promptly pulled it into his mouth, and both Ruby and Jake laughed.

Now that Ruby was here, she wasn't at all sure she should have come. It wasn't just her weekend she was exploding by this interruption—it was Aaron's time off, as well. He deserved a couple of days a week when she wasn't hovering over him, barking out commands, didn't he?

"You're here for your marine?" Jake guessed, his eyes twinkling suggestively.

"He's not my marine," she said, scoffing at Jake and wishing he wouldn't look at her as if there was something going on between her and Aaron. "I don't really know why I've come. This was probably a bad idea. I don't want to bother him on his day off."

Jake lifted an eyebrow. "Bother him? Yeah, no. I don't think so. He's in the kitchen, in case you're interested."

Ruby chuckled. "Now, why am I not surprised?" Aaron was a large man with a similarly big appetite. "Midday snack?"

Jake burst out a laugh. "Something like that."

Weird.

Then again, in Ruby's opinion, Jake had always had an expansive personality. But as long as he was good to Avery, Ruby was happy.

Jake didn't have to point her way to the kitchen. She'd helped her sister remodel the place when she first bought it, and she knew where everything was located. This wasn't just any old bed-and-breakfast. It was Jake and Avery's heartfelt contribution to A New Leash on Love. This was where potential clients came to stay while they trained with their new service dogs. It offered them escape from having to worry about finding housing or most of their meals. Breakfast and lunch were provided, and there were plenty of delicious fixin's for easy dinners stocked in the refrigerator and pantry—not to mention some wonderful restaurants to visit in Whispering Pines.

Avery was the business side of the Winslows' companies and took care of the paperwork and accounting. Jake had found his place in the Winslows' ministry, cooking for his guests at the B and B, and then Jake and Avery shared the cleaning duties and child-care between them. In addition to baby Felix, Jake had a five-year-old daughter named Lottie, whom Avery had adopted as her own soon after their marriage.

Waving a thank-you to Jake, Ruby turned the corner into the kitchen, expecting to see Aaron at the kitchen table nomming on a snack.

She couldn't have been more wrong.

Aaron stood at the counter, his back to her, humming under his breath. It wasn't a song she recognized. Maybe it wasn't even a song at all, as it didn't follow any kind of pattern Ruby could discern. Though she couldn't see it past his broad shoulders, she heard the buzz of an electric mixer in the background. Various baking items—bins of flour and sugar, sticks of butter and a gallon of milk—were spread out on the counter next to him.

Was he *baking*?

It wasn't that she held any old-fashioned notions that men never baked. Jake did all the cooking here at the bed-and-breakfast, and he was a guy. It was specifically Aaron who'd surprised her. His obvious familiarity in the kitchen was just *so* not the rough-and-ready marine with whom Ruby was familiar that she almost didn't believe her eyes. She nearly pinched herself just to make sure she hadn't dreamed all this up.

At least Aaron had Oscar with him. The black poodle was sheltered under the breakfast nook, napping with his chin on his paws, looking entirely content just hanging out with his person.

"Aaron?" she asked tentatively as she entered the room.

He swung around so fast that the mint-green frosting on the spatula he was holding—now rather like a weapon—went flinging across the room, a couple of large chunks of the soft, fluffy cream landing in Ruby's hair.

His expression immediately went from one of utter shock and surprise to—what?

Embarrassment?

Chagrin?

"Ruby! What are you…?"

"Is this how you spend your Saturday afternoons?" she asked, picking at the frosting in her hair and feeling at least as stunned as he must be. "I never would have guessed in a million years that you were a closet chef. Whatcha baking?"

"I—er—" he stammered. Without answering, he whipped the dish towel from off his shoulder and fruitlessly dabbed at her hair, his face turning bright red under a couple of days' scruff.

And speaking of red…

"I must look like a Christmas tree right now, between my red hair and the green frosting. All I need is a string of lights and I'll be good to go."

"I am so sorry." He continued to apologize profusely as he scrubbed and dabbed at her hair with his towel—rather ineffectively, were she to guess. She could feel the frosting spreading across her scalp and could only begin to picture what a sight she must look like right now.

Laughing, she grabbed his wrists and twisted away from him to stop him from continuing the pointless behavior. "Aaron, please. You're only making it worse!"

He immediately dropped his hands, and his face became even more flushed, if that were possible. "You're right. I'm just mashing it in. I'm sorry. I'm afraid you're going to need a shower after this. My bad."

He looked so mortified that she couldn't help but laugh. "No worries. It's nothing a little shampoo won't fix. Now tell me about—" she gestured, first toward him and then toward the mixer "—this."

With a reluctant groan, he turned his attention back to the counter and set the spatula back in the mixing bowl.

"Cupcakes," he said, his low, raspy baritone voice indicating such an admission was beneath him.

"Really?" She wondered if she sounded as stunned as she was feeling right now. Her eyes must be huge. Everything she'd seen since she'd entered the bed-and-breakfast today was a contradiction in terms.

"Avery and Jake have new guests coming in this week, and I thought I would bake up some cupcakes for them to enjoy. It seems like the least I can do after all they've done for me. They've been fantastic, and I—er—baking is one of my few hobbies."

Ruby slid onto a stool next to the island counter and propped her chin on her palms. "Please…don't let me stop you. I love cupcakes. What flavor are you making?"

He turned and leaned his hip against the counter, crossing his arms and tilting his head as he narrowed his gaze on her. "Yellow cake with cream cheese frosting. Why? What is your favorite?"

She grinned at him. "Yellow cake with cream cheese frosting." She gave him a casual shrug. "If they're any good."

"Hmmph. Be prepared to be amazed."

He turned back to the counter and flipped on the mixer, humming off-key, as he'd been doing when she'd first walked in.

She watched him in silence, enjoying the rare sight of a true man's man who knew his way around the kitchen. There was something just so incredibly attractive about the dish towel slung over his broad shoulder, his deep, tuneless humming and the way his biceps tightened under the sleeves of his black T-shirt as he measured and poured.

The butterflies suddenly loosed in her stomach put her on edge.

What was she thinking?

Or maybe that was the problem.

She *wasn't* thinking.

She was feeling. Leaning in with her heart and not her head. And she needed to stamp out that little spark before it flamed into a fire, because she suddenly realized it could potentially happen despite her father and her past relationship with Daniel.

Aaron held the key to opening up a whole new world for her and the family's service-dog business. She didn't dare mess it up by becoming personally involved with him in any way. No. She reminded herself that she would *never* become involved with a military man—not after living through what war had done to Daniel and her own father.

Still—objectively speaking, Aaron was a good-looking man. As long as she kept her heart locked up and her eyeballs in her head, she should be good to go.

Aaron poured the cupcake batter into a couple of muffin pans and slid them into the oven. His work for the moment finished, he then pulled up a stool next to her and half perched on it, leaning on his elbow as he captured Ruby's gaze.

"So, tell me—if you didn't come by this afternoon to sample my culinary wares, why are you here?"

Aaron was curious to find out the answer to his question, but it was more to change her focus than anything.

Talk about humiliating.

There was no reason whatsoever for him to feel ashamed. She probably would have found out about it via Jake and Avery if she hadn't walked in on him herself. Half of the reason he was baking today was that Ruby's brother-in-law Jake had talked him into it. They'd become good friends since Aaron had moved into the B and B. Aaron could relate to Jake, and they'd spent many evenings together shooting the breeze. Jake wasn't a wimp by any means. He was large and extroverted, with a strong handshake and a huge grin. When he'd married Ruby's sister Avery, he'd embraced a life of service, taking care of the bed-and-breakfast—including doing all the cooking.

It didn't seem to bother him—or his masculinity—one bit.

So, Aaron didn't know why his ego felt stung that Ruby had walked in on him. Maybe it was because he was baking cupcakes he was planning on frosting mint green.

Whatever it was, he was struggling with his emotions.

And then he was hoping Ruby didn't notice he was struggling.

"Did you need me for something?" he asked and then realized his question sounded a little self-centered. "Oh. Of course, you're not here for me. You're probably here to visit your sister and niece and nephew, right?"

She raised her eyebrows. "No," she said softly, drawing out the word. "I'm here to see you."

His heart jumped into his throat and started hammering mercilessly. He felt almost as if he were back in high school, and the girl on whom he'd had a crush had just looked his direction.

"Okay. What do you need me to do?" Presumably, it had something to do with his service-dog training. Or maybe she needed a favor. A leaky faucet or something, although she had two brothers on the farm, not to mention a gaggle of sisters, who could do that sort of thing—or Ruby could do it herself. She was quite self-sufficient.

"Nothing," she finally answered.

Now it was his turn to raise a brow.

"That's pretty cryptic," he pointed out.

"Right. No. I don't need anything from you. I just stopped by to see how you were getting along. I thought maybe you'd be bored or something since you don't have to train today. I guess I shouldn't have worried on that score, huh?"

She'd been worried about him?

He couldn't remember the last time anyone had cared enough to check up on him, even if it was only to make sure he wasn't bored out of his mind.

"I'll leave you to your baking. I can see I'm in your way," she continued, standing as if to leave.

"No, not at all," he answered so fast his brain had to catch up to his mouth. He reached out and gently grabbed her hand to keep her from walking away. "You're here. Why don't you stay and have a cupcake?"

She shrugged nonchalantly and sat back down on the stool, but the sparkle in her light blue eyes matched her smile. "Well, if you insist. I was always the taste tester for my mom when I was a kid. You know—the one who hung around the kitchen just to be able to lick the spatula?"

He glanced at the counter where he'd placed the smaller mixing bowl filled with frosting and the accompanying spatula. Everything else he'd used so far was in the sink, soaking in hot, soapy water.

"I didn't even think to offer it to you."

She chuckled. "It isn't as if I would have taken it even if you had."

"Why not? After I finish frosting the cupcakes, the spatula is yours," he assured her.

"Hey, now. I have dignity, even if most of the time you can't tell. I'm trying to present myself as a grown woman here—although I'll admit it may be difficult to do so with mint-green frosting in my hair." She tilted her chin and huffed dramatically.

She had no idea what he really thought of her. There was no question in Aaron's mind that Ruby was 100 percent an attrac-

tive woman. That was half his problem—
the other half being the ridiculous dog she'd
paired him with.

The oven timer went off, and Aaron was
grateful for a moment to catch his breath.
He opened the oven and set the cupcakes on
a cooling rack.

"I've got half an hour to kill before I can
frost them. Do you want to get a breath of
fresh air?"

She hopped off the stool, and Tugger immediately moved to her heel. "I thought you'd
never ask. As wonderful as those cupcakes
smell, it's too nice of a day to spend the whole
day in the kitchen. I was on cleaning duty this
morning at the house and didn't even get out
to play with the dogs."

He liked that she was an outdoorsy type
like he was. More often than not, when he arrived at A New Leash on Love in the morn-
ings, Ruby would already be outside, running
dogs through the agility course or cheerfully
cleaning the dog pen.

"Oscar, heel," he commanded the poodle—
his poodle, he reminded himself when Oscar
immediately obeyed him, and he slipped him
a treat. He didn't know if the poodle's com-
panionship would ever feel natural to him,

although he was becoming more used to the dog as the days went by.

"We have to let the cupcakes cool down a bit before Aaron can frost them," Ruby told Jake as they passed through the living room.

Jake was slowly rocking back and forth in a chair with a now-sleeping Felix curled on his shoulder.

"Don't freak out if you happen to see the mess in the kitchen," Aaron whispered so the baby wouldn't wake up. "I'll clean it up when I come back in."

"No worries. Have fun, kids," Jake said with a low snicker.

When they were outside, Ruby turned to Aaron and rolled her eyes. "Honestly, I don't know how Avery puts up with Jake sometimes. She's so serious-minded and he's loud and gregarious. It would drive me crazy. But as long as he makes her happy, I suppose that's all that matters."

"To each his own," Aaron quipped lightly, but his gut flipped when his gaze met and locked with Ruby's and realized Ruby had heard and interpreted it in a totally different way than what he'd meant.

"I believe that—that God has a special someone meant just for me. Don't you?" Her voice was soft, and she suddenly sounded shy.

He supposed he believed God made one woman for one man. He'd heard people talk about finding their person. But because of his choice in career, he hadn't ever really given it much thought. He knew how difficult military spouses had it and would never wish that on his worst enemy, much less someone he loved, so it had simply never been an issue. While he'd dated now and again when he wasn't on one of his tours, he'd never even looked for a serious relationship.

"I didn't mean—" he started.

"No. I know." She cut him off and changed the subject. "So, where do you want to go? There are a couple of easy hiking paths with trailheads that start right around the back of the cabin or else I can borrow Avery's truck to drive us to town or something if you just want to walk around and browse the shops."

Neither one of those options really appealed to Aaron right now. He would never admit how hard he had to struggle just to take a simple hike, and quite honestly, he appreciated having the weekend off to recuperate. And he definitely didn't care for the idea of strolling around town window-shopping.

He was a guy. He hated shopping—or *browsing*, as she'd called it.

"I'd just as soon stick around here, if that's

okay with you. I know I already told Jake I'd take care of the mess in the kitchen, but I don't know what he'll think if I take off, especially if we borrow their truck."

"At least it's a truck—something appropriate to drive on mountain roads. Believe it or not, Jake rented a bright red Mustang when he first came to town." Ruby gestured toward the porch swing.

He held his breath as he sat down, feeling suddenly unstable on his legs. He wasn't sure whether that had more to do with his injury or that he was here with Ruby. She had the strangest effect on him.

"Now, why doesn't that surprise me?" Aaron chuckled as he pictured Jake tooling around in the most inappropriate car for the area he could possibly imagine, what with all the hairpin curves and dirt roads. What would be the point of driving a sports car around here?

"And you've gotten to know what a crazy personality Jake has since you've been here. He drove it like a maniac, of course."

"Of course. Is there any other way to drive a sports car?"

"Not with Jake, apparently. But I don't really want to talk about Jake and Avery." She settled back onto the porch swing and pulled in one of her legs, wrapping her arms around her knee so she could turn toward him.

"Okay." He leaned forward and stared at the floor, bracing his forearms on his legs and locking his fingers together.

He expected her to jump in with whatever was on her mind, as she usually did, but she didn't say a word, and the uncomfortable silence between them lingered. Or at least, the silence was uncomfortable for him. Though he wasn't looking at her, he felt as if she was staring at him, and it made him twitchy.

He scoured his mind for something to say, but he came up with a big blank.

Talking was hard.

Especially with Ruby. He felt the need to impress her and instead wasn't even able to come up with two words to put together. He wished she would speak first.

"Tell me more about yourself," she said at last, her curiosity obvious.

He bolted upward, his spine stiffening. This was way worse than the silence. He hated talking about himself.

"Like what?" he asked apprehensively. He really wasn't into *sharing*.

"Well, let's see. I know you were a sergeant in the marines and served several tours in

Afghanistan. Thank you for your service, by the way. Major respect."

He jerked a quick nod, always uncomfortable when people acknowledged the work he'd done in the military, though he supposed he appreciated that people cared that someone was out there serving the country and keeping them safe.

"After watching you with Oscar—well, I can picture you commanding your troops. It's no wonder you rose to the rank of sergeant. You seem to me to be a natural leader."

He had been—once. He wasn't anything now. It was a struggle just to get up in the morning, and it was all he could do not to cringe when he thought about how much his life had changed.

"Was it hard—leading men into battle?" she tentatively asked, her voice smooth and gentle. She paused and shook her head. "No, I'm sorry. You don't have to answer that if you don't want to. It was wrong of me to ask."

He wasn't offended by her question, and he sat back, catching her gaze. "It was my job. My duty," he answered. "To bring all my men home safely."

Her expression softened as she continued to stare at him. "I can tell honor means a lot to you."

"My marines meant a lot to me."

"That's how you were injured, right? I read the reports. You threw yourself on top of one of the marines under your command during an explosion."

As always happened when Aaron thought back to that moment, a sharp blade stabbed between his ribs. He wouldn't have changed what he'd done in that second, nor would he pat himself on the back for doing what, to him, had been automatic and not something for which to win special honors, but that was also the moment that had changed the entire trajectory of his life.

He hated that part of the story—the part that would drag on and on for the rest of his life.

"I... Can we not talk about me?" He felt as if he were begging and hoped it didn't sound that way to Ruby. That was all he needed.

"I'm so sorry. Of course, this is a sensitive subject for you. I apologize for even bringing it up. I just thought I might be able to better understand where you're coming from if I heard the story from you. You know. For our training."

"I was an active marine in a firefight." His voice was low and raspy as he forced out the words. "Now I'm not."

Chapter Seven

"So, why do you do what you do?" Aaron asked, clearly trying to change the subject and get the spotlight off him.

Not that Ruby could blame him. She couldn't even begin to imagine what he'd been through defending the country. No wonder he didn't want to talk about it.

"What I do...? You mean, training my service dogs?"

"For veterans," he specified. "Why do you want this so bad?"

"Oh." She paused as her heart clenched. "That."

"Is it because of your dad and Daniel? I figure there must be some specific reason why you're chasing after this military contract. Honestly, most people don't think that much about veterans. If you were anyone else, I'd think trying to get a contract such as this is probably for the influx of government money, but I've been around you long enough to recognize that's not you—or your program."

"No. You already know me well enough to know money has very little to do with the way I live my life." She chuckled. "Which is a good thing, since I don't have much of it. Everything goes into my dogs. But I have to admit money does come into play this time."

"Is A New Leash on Love hurting financially? Wait…no. You don't have to answer that."

She stared off into the forest. "It's becoming more and more difficult to make ends meet," she said. "This is a ministry, and we don't charge for our service dogs."

"But even ministries need money, especially those who have hungry pups to feed."

"It's not something I like to think about. But it can't be avoided. And when the possibility of attaining a lucrative military contract came around, it seemed like a blessing from God."

"I imagine so."

"Our program has assisted a lot of people, from children to the elderly, with a variety of different needs, both physical and mental, but helping veterans has always been something close to my heart because—"

She paused, choking up as tears burned in her eyes. She didn't want to cry in front of him, but she didn't know how she was going to get through this story dry-eyed. She'd thought she was many years beyond tears on this subject, but with Aaron...

He pressed a gentle hand onto her shoulder and rubbed it lightly. She'd thought maybe he was going to try to scramble back out of this conversation as quick as he could. Tears were no doubt the last thing he'd expected— or wanted.

So, she was surprised when his large hand moved to frame her cheek and he murmured, "It's okay. Take your time. I'm here for you."

She needed to talk to him, to get this out of her system. It wasn't something she'd ever shared with anyone, not even her siblings, and it was eating away at her. She hadn't realized how much until just this minute.

"I told you about my father," she finally said, choking out the words. "And you met Daniel."

"Your high school boyfriend."

"That's right. I'm not sure why he enlisted, but he was gung ho to join up even before he graduated from high school. I'll be honest with you. Granted, we were just kids, but we'd been dating since we were freshmen, and I thought it was serious. But when he enlisted, I felt as if he didn't give me a second thought. When he returned, we tried to strike up our relationship again, but he was angry all the time and he frightened me. We fought all the time and eventually broke up. Right after that, he was arrested. He hijacked a car and was caught with drugs on him.

"He seems to be doing much better now, though. I'm glad to see him back in church."

Aaron grunted and broke eye contact, looking just over her shoulder, his jaw tightly clenched, and she felt as if she'd hit a nerve.

"I'm sorry. I've been going on and on without thinking about how you must feel about it. Do you want to talk about something else?" she asked.

He vehemently shook his head. "Not on my account."

"I feel as if I'm upsetting you," she pressed.

He smiled at her, but it didn't reach his brown eyes. "You're right. I'm upset. But not because of you. I promise. Not even because of what you told me."

He stopped then and stared off into the distance.

"What is it, then?" she asked after a quiet moment.

"I understand Daniel better than I'd like to admit. I wanted to be a marine from the time I was a little boy, seeing those television commercials with the men in their dress blues, holding a sword. You know. 'The few. The proud. The marines.'"

"I can see where there would be an attraction," she said. "It was part of what I had to come to terms with after Daniel left. I expect many little boys feel an attraction to the military lifestyle—and young men, for that matter."

He shrugged. "Yeah. Maybe. Little guys playing with plastic army men. But I think part of it is that I was raised by a single mom. I never knew my dad and had no uncles or anything to be a good male role model for me. Poor Mom. I was the bane of her existence growing up."

"How so?"

"Any way I could get into trouble, I did. Bad grades, calls to the principal's office, smoking behind the house, shoplifting stupid stuff just because I could. So, when the US Marine Corps enlistment representatives set up a booth at our high school career fair, I spent a lot of time talking to them. It didn't take much convincing on my part, but I thought for sure my mom would nix the idea when I brought her home a brochure."

"I take it she didn't?"

He coughed out a dry laugh. "Just the opposite. She encouraged me to enlist. Said maybe it would help me grow up and become a man."

Ruby smiled. "And did it?"

"Let's just say it didn't take long for me to learn not to talk back. Drill sergeants have a way of intimidating even the mouthiest of boys. But yes, the marines instilled me with a sense of purpose, honor and pride I'd been missing from my life. The day I completed the Crucible and received my eagle, globe and anchor was truly the best day of my life."

"You were born to be a marine." The moment the words were out of her mouth, she wished them back, but it was too late for that. His face had already turned into a hard, emotionless mask.

He scoffed. "Ironic, isn't it?"

"Aaron, you're still a marine. You always will be. What is it they say? 'Once a marine, always a marine'?"

He shook his head. "In name only. That's what bothers me the most. I didn't just have a job—I had a calling. I knew who I was and what I was supposed to do with my life every morning when I woke up. Now? I don't even know how to make it through today, much less the future. It's just a wide, blank canvas full of nothing."

She thought she understood, at least a little, how it must be for him now. It must be frightening for a man like Aaron to suddenly encounter such changes. His whole life had gone from solving problems and getting it done to suddenly being virtually abandoned.

Thank you for your service. Have a good day.

"Maybe it's a good thing to be looking at your future as if it were a blank canvas," she suggested somewhat warily, not sure how he'd take it since he'd already brought it up. "Ready for you to paint on?"

"I can't paint," he said in a raspy monotone.

"You know that's not what I meant."

He shook his head. "No. I know. I don't mean to take it out on you. It's not your fault I'm half a man."

"You're all man to me," she said, feeling the heat rise to her face when a half smile curled on his lips. At least she'd gotten a smile out of him, however wry, even if it was at the cost of her own complete mortification. "I— er—don't take that the wrong way. What I meant was there are so many things out there you can do to help yourself and others, to find a new meaning and purpose for your life. God hasn't deserted you, you know."

His brow lowered. "Hasn't He?"

"No." Her answer was firm, as was her belief. "He's just set you on a different path, one you'll have to discover as you go along, starting with learning how to live with your service dog. I can imagine how difficult this whole process has been for you, and yet you've already come so far in just two weeks of this program. Life can be like that for you, as well."

She could tell he didn't believe a word of what she was saying, and there was no way she was going to convince him. The best thing she could do for him right now was pray that in the same way he was discovering success in her program, he'd find his life's purpose, with the Lord's help.

Her words were clearly having no effect on him, but God could work where man could not.

"Have the cupcakes cooled down yet?" she asked him, her voice gentle as she pulled him away from the deep conversation.

He checked his watch—a tactical military watch, not a fitness brand.

"Yep," he said gruffly. At the sound of his voice, Oscar lifted his head and tilted it at him, quietly whining.

"Oscar hears the stress in your tone," Ruby explained.

"Hmm. He'd better get used to it," he muttered.

Ruby reached out and squeezed Aaron's hand but immediately dropped it when he pulled away.

"Come on," he said. "Let's go back in and finish the job."

Aaron reached for the bowl of frosting, adjusting it back into the mixer and expertly whipping the mint-green frosting into light points so it would be easy to spread across the cupcakes.

Ruby remained silent as Aaron worked, which suited him just fine. As far as he was concerned, he was all talked out and then some. It wasn't that he didn't like Ruby—he did. But she always managed to get underneath his skin, make him think hard thoughts. He didn't want to do that right now—or ever, really, if he was being honest. It was easier not to consider his life than to try to figure things out.

If he attempted to paint on his life's canvas

as she'd suggested, he already knew what the result would be. It would turn into a mess of colors that would look like a kindergartner's finger painting.

A big blob of nothing.

So instead, he concentrated on his cupcakes. Cupcakes, he could do and do well, even in his perpetually weakened state. Using his spatula, he scooped frosting into a pastry bag with a frosting tip.

"Do you want to help?" he asked her as he transferred the cupcakes to the center aisle, where she was propped on a stool, watching him.

"Oh, no, no. You don't want me touching your beautiful cupcake masterpieces. Baking is definitely not my forte. Eating, on the other hand… These look awesome. How about I be your taste tester instead? I'm totally willing to help out there."

He chuckled, despite his foul mood. "Deal," he told her, holding a cupcake in one hand while expertly smoothing the mint frosting across the top with the tip of the bag.

He reached out, offering it to her, noticing the pretty flush of her cheeks and the shine in her blue eyes as she took the cupcake from him with a gracious nod.

"If this tastes as good as it looks, I'm in for a real treat."

"Stop talking and start eating," he teased. She was going to give him a big head with all her praise.

"Gladly." She unwrapped the cupcake and dove in, taking a large bite that encompassed both cake and frosting. "Mmm," she said as she chewed. "Mmm, mmm, mmm."

He chuckled again, amused by her blatant enthusiasm. She was as eager as a preschooler—and she had a dollop of frosting on one of her cheeks.

"Good gracious, Aaron. They ought to be patented, they're so good."

"I always told my grandmother that."

"You learned well."

He cleared his throat, uncomfortable with her admiration but smiling, nonetheless. "I— you have—" He brushed a hand over the scruff on his cheek, indicating where she should dab on her own cheek.

She swiped at the frosting but missed.

"Did I get it?" She tilted her head so he could better see.

He grinned and shook his head.

Their eyes met and locked, and his gut tightened. He didn't have the foggiest notion what to do with the emotions he was feeling right now, only that avoiding the sparkle in her eyes by dropping his gaze to her smiling lips turned out *not* to be the best idea he'd ever had.

His gaze shot back up. Her eyes had darkened to the deepest blue, the color of the middle of the ocean, and her smile was somehow different than it had been just seconds before.

"Do you mind if I…?" he asked, surprised at how deep his voice sounded. He gestured toward her cheek.

"Of course." She leaned forward, so close to him their breaths mingled.

He stopped breathing altogether as he reached out and tenderly brushed the frosting from her soft skin.

There was a long, intense moment when neither of them moved nor said a word, the air between them so thick it was almost palpable.

When his eyes returned to her lips, he had the sudden and nearly impossible to resist impulse to kiss her. If he leaned in just the tiniest bit—or if she did, for that matter—their lips would touch.

He'd never wanted anything so badly in his life. This was all new territory to him. He wasn't a teenager now, yet he felt the same kind of awkwardness as he had back in high school when he'd shared his first kiss with a girl at a school dance.

He was a full-grown man who didn't know what he was doing other than following the directions of his heart.

They were close—so close. His gaze locked on Ruby's lips.

Then she stood abruptly and the stool nearly shot out from under her.

"It seems unfair that you'd keep such a wonderful secret all to yourself." Her words tumbled out in a rush, her voice high and threaded like a harp. "Have you ever thought about selling them?"

"What?" he asked, totally disoriented. He'd been so wrapped up in the moment, his heart rapidly hammering in his chest, that he felt as if she'd yanked the rug out from under him and he'd taken a bad fall. He'd clearly done something wrong but had no idea what.

Had he misread all her signs?

"Have you ever considered selling your cupcakes?" she repeated. "If you ask me, it would be a great first start on painting that new life canvas of yours."

"Cupcakes? Not a chance," he said without even giving it a thought—which was good because his brain was still completely muddled.

"Why not?" she demanded, propping one fist on her hip and raising an eyebrow.

Were they really having this conversation about *cupcakes*? Hadn't she been feeling the same thing he had only moments before? Or had it all been on his end? He was so confused right now he barely knew up from down or right from left.

"Because I'm a guy," he finally said, as if that explained everything.

She chuckled, but it sounded kind of *off*, as if her throat had closed around the vibration. "As if that makes the least bit of sense. What does the fact that you're a man have to do with baking and selling cupcakes?"

"Don't tell me you weren't surprised when you first walked in on me baking. That's just not my thing. It was embarrassing enough to have you come in and catch me indulging in my guilty pleasure." He wished she wouldn't press him on this, but that wasn't Ruby's style. She'd just keep pushing until she got the answer she wanted.

"That's just weird and you know it. Many of the world's best chefs are men. Jake doesn't freak out when people find out he cooks for the bed-and-breakfast."

"Be that as it may, it's not for me."

She paused for a moment, considering.

"What if we kept it anonymous?" she suggested, tilting her head as she regarded him. "I would absolutely love to put some of these in the Winslow's Woodlands gift shop if you wouldn't mind baking a dozen or so every other day. I know that'll take away some of your free time in the evenings, but just think about what you'll accomplish if you do. You said yourself you really enjoy baking, and we won't be able to keep them stocked." She chuckled. "In fact, once Sharpe gets a taste of one of these, he'll buy up the whole dozen every time we put them out on the shelf."

"I don't know." It wasn't that he minded baking the cupcakes. It would give him something to do to help him not dwell on himself—or Ruby. "Wouldn't I be in the way here at the bed-and-breakfast? What would Jake think?"

"What would Jake think about what?" asked Jake, entering the kitchen with Felix tucked under his arm like a football. He was immediately sidetracked by the cupcakes on the counter and headed straight for them. "May I?" he asked, his hand hovering over the platter.

"Yeah, of course," Aaron answered, gesturing toward the goodies. "Help yourself."

Jake used his teeth to undo the wrapping

enough to take a bite. One bite…two…and the cupcake was gone. The only hint that he'd eaten a cupcake at all was Jake's mint-green lips grinning back at them.

"That was absolutely awesome," Jake enthused. "Where did you learn how to bake, buddy? In the marines?"

That set Ruby into giggles. Otherwise, Aaron realized he might have felt offended before thinking it through and recognizing Jake's joke for what it was. He really needed to work on his worldview. If hanging out with Ruby had taught him anything, it was that he was too stiff-necked about just about everything in his life.

He took a deep breath and tried to relax and let the tension wash over him.

Jake had evidently finally looked over at Ruby and noticed the frosting in her hair, because he threw back his head and bellowed with laughter. "What happened to you?"

Her lips curled into a smile. "Mint-green frosting happened to me. Obviously."

"Do I dare ask?"

"Long story short, I startled Aaron when I first entered the kitchen this afternoon. He was armed with a spatula full of green frosting."

Jake grinned. "Sounds dangerous."

"I'm trying to convince him to sell his cup-cakes at our farm," Ruby explained, clearly trying to get Jake's attention off her Christmas-colored hair. "But he's still kind of iffy about it. What's your take on the subject?"

"The world would really lose out if he *didn't* sell them," Jake said. "We've got to convince him this is what he ought to be doing with his free time here—and that he needs to leave at least a few around the B and B whenever he bakes."

Aaron noticed that they were speaking about him in the third person as if he wasn't even in the room.

"Hello," Aaron said, stepping into the conversation. "I'm standing right here."

"Of course, you are." Jake thudded him on the back, nearly sending him off-kilter, and Aaron wasn't a small man by any means. Thankfully, Oscar was at Aaron's side and immediately leaned into him, keeping him on his feet. "But really. The world needs your cupcakes. They just do."

"Yeah, I don't know," Aaron said, drag-ging his proverbial feet. "I'd have to use your kitchen, and I'd just be in your way all the time."

"No, you wouldn't," Jake and Ruby said

simultaneously, and then they both looked at each other and laughed.

"We don't serve dinner, remember?" Jake reminded him. "It's not like you'll be in my way or anything. My poor little kitchen is just waiting to be used in the evenings."

Jake's *little* kitchen was actually industrial-sized, as well he knew. They could probably cook in this enormous kitchen at the same time and not be in each other's way.

Aaron looked from one to the other of them and knew he wasn't going to get out of this unscathed. And it wasn't as if he didn't enjoy baking. It was the only hobby he had that really calmed him down and gave him a sense of peace in his life. If he anonymously donated the cupcakes for sale at Winslow's with the stipulation that the money went into the military service-dog program, wouldn't he be doing a good thing for everyone concerned?

Finally, he shrugged. "Yeah. Okay. I suppose I can bake a few dozen for Winslow's Woodlands while I'm staying here. Where and when do you want them delivered?"

Ruby cheered and did a little victory dance that made Aaron chuckle.

"Just bring them with you to training when you come, and I'll take care of the rest," she told him. "I'm so excited about your new endeavor. This is going to be great."

"But be sure to leave a couple behind," Jake reminded him. "We'll consider that to be payment for using my kitchen."

"Done," said Aaron just as Jake's little girl raced into the kitchen, sliding on her socks across the wood-paneled floor as she swung her arms around Ruby.

"Auntie Ruby! Auntie Ruby!" she exclaimed. "I didn't know you were here."

"I would have come around and said hi to you in a minute, pumpkin. I was busy talking to your daddy and Sergeant Jamison," Ruby said.

"But I want you more than they do," little five-year-old Lottie demanded in a whiny voice that suggested perhaps she might benefit from a nap. "Daddy and Sarge can play by themselves."

Everyone chuckled and Ruby lifted a brow at Aaron. "'Sarge'?"

"It works." His face heated as he shrugged, and he rubbed a palm across his scruff. From the beginning, Lottie had stuck that nickname on him. She'd tried *Sergeant*, but it didn't quite roll off her tongue, and then Jake had suggested *Sarge* and that was it.

"Lottie, why don't we go into the living

room and let your daddy and Sarge play in the kitchen for a bit?" Ruby suggested, unable to keep the giggle from her voice. "Jake, do you want me to take baby Felix for you?"

"Actually," said Jake, "I have a special favor to ask of Aaron."

Aaron smiled. It appeared that was something he did more often these days. He wasn't sure when that had started happening, but suddenly grinning almost seemed second nature to him. "Sure. Whatever you need."

"Can you watch Felix for a few minutes?"

Wait, what?

His heart hammered to attention and then stopped beating altogether as confusion and anxiety washed over him.

"I don't understand. Ruby just volunteered her services where Felix is concerned. I know she wants to hold the baby," he protested. "I feel as if I'd be depriving her of her auntie status, and I don't want to do that."

"Yes, but I'm not asking her to hold the baby. I'm asking you."

The grin dropped from Aaron's face.

What was this?

"Why?" he demanded, narrowing his eyes on Jake and feeling cornered.

"Because you, Sergeant Jamison, need to

learn how to hold a baby. And what better time than now?"

Now, why would Jake think he needed to learn a social skill like how to hold a baby? That wasn't the sort of thing a man such as he would ever have reason to need to know. He wasn't going to marry, and he didn't have siblings, so he wouldn't be a father and becoming an uncle was out of the question. His future was no doubt going to be lonely and grim.

He wouldn't wish spending a lifetime with his broken self on his worst enemy, much less on the woman he loved. It was bad enough knowing he wasn't husband material without thinking about the fact that he was the last Jamison male in his family. He wouldn't be passing on his name to his children the way Jake had done with Lottie and Felix. He would never hold a baby of his own and hence didn't need to practice with Felix.

It wasn't even something he'd ever given much thought to until this moment.

He held up both hands, palms out as if in surrender. "You really don't want me to do that," he assured Jake. "I'm far too clumsy to hold a baby."

Jake snickered. "Yeah, right. You were a sniper in the marine corps and could hold yourself completely still for hours, but you can't hold a baby for just a few minutes?"

"Felix wiggles. And he might break."

"He won't break," Aaron heard Ruby's cheery voice sounding her opinion from the living room. Apparently, she'd been eavesdropping on this entire extremely uncomfortable conversation. She appeared in the kitchen moments later, holding a plastic teacup in one hand and draped in a pink scarf.

"Felix is tougher than he appears," Jake agreed with a wink. "This pudgy little guy has enough padding to keep him perfectly safe with you. Besides, I trust you."

Aaron's gut tightened.

Jake trusted him.

Ruby trusted him.

The problem was he didn't trust himself. He'd seen Felix pump his little legs up and down when he got excited. What if that happened while Aaron was holding him?

No. He had to find an excuse to get out of it.

"What about the dogs?" He didn't know why he thought that excuse was going to work, seeing as this whole setup at the bed-and-breakfast was based around training service dogs. "Who is going to watch over them while we take care of the kids?"

"Command Oscar to go out with Tugger," Ruby said, holding open the kitchen door that led to a fenced area out back.

Surely Oscar would have listened to Ruby should she have said the word, but Aaron supposed he appreciated that she was trying not to step on his toes during training. Oscar was his dog now, so he bid the poodle to go outside. He didn't have to worry about whether or not the dog would listen to him, and the thought surprised him. He and Oscar had come further than he'd thought.

"Well, then," Jake said. "No more excuses. Baby time."

"I—er, okay," Aaron said. He knew when he was being ganged up on, but there was no help for it. Jake would have been formidable by himself, but with Ruby at his side, there was no way Aaron was coming out of this unscathed. He only hoped Felix would be more fortunate.

Unsure of what to do next, Aaron held both arms straight out, palms up and as stiff as a log. Jake was carrying his kid around like a football. Aaron thought he might be able to do a little better than that.

"Relax," Jake coached. "This really is easier than it looks."

"Says you," Aaron muttered under his

breath. "You're an expert on the subject. You have two kids."

"Well, I didn't always have kids. Once upon a time, I held a baby for the first time, and she was a lot smaller and more fragile than this big guy is."

"Hmm."

"And I had to learn how to be an auntie," Ruby added from just behind Aaron's shoulder. He'd thought she'd returned to the living room, and it startled him.

"Relax your arms," she instructed, following her words by running her palm across his tight shoulders. "Remember to breathe. Jake's going to hand Felix to you now. Just lay him against your shoulder. Keep one arm underneath him and the other on his back."

Aaron gritted his teeth. "What if he wiggles?"

"You're stronger than he is," she pointed out with a giggle.

"Exactly my point. What if I squeeze him too hard?" His throat closed around his voice, making it sound squeaky.

"You won't."

This was worse than when he'd first set eyes on Oscar. He'd had no idea what to do with a froufrou dog, but that was nothing at all compared to holding a baby.

Jake grinned and held Felix out to him. Aaron's stomach turned over. It was saying something that Jake trusted Aaron with his son, especially knowing how inexperienced he was. But for some reason, Jake was pushing this on him.

Taking a deep breath, Aaron grasped nine-month-old Felix around his rib cage and quickly brought the baby to his shoulder, tucking him close and following the instructions Ruby had given him.

"See?" Ruby beamed at him. "That wasn't so difficult, now, was it?"

He begged to differ with her but knew it wouldn't do any good, so he simply turned and walked into the living room, searching for the best place to sit down as quickly as he could. There was a wooden rocker, but Aaron was aiming for the most stability possible with a baby in his arms, so he decided on a stiff-backed chair. Lottie was in the middle of the room, setting up a tea party on the coffee table with a couple of dolls and a few stuffed animals in tow.

"Would you like some tea, Sarge?" she asked politely, holding out a plastic cup after pouring the "tea" from a toy teapot. She walked up to him and extended the cup with one hand while wrapping a purple scarf around his neck with the other. Felix got a blue scarf around his waist.

Aaron tried not to fidget with the scarf, even if it wasn't exactly his color of choice. He didn't have the slightest idea how he was going to hold a baby and drink tea—even pretend tea—at the same time, but he didn't want to hurt the little girl's feelings.

"Yes, please. That sounds wonderful," he said, forcing a smile to his lips and taking the cup from her. He hoped Lottie couldn't tell how strained his voice was or how quickly he set the cup down on a nearby end table once it was in his grasp.

Ruby certainly noticed. Her gaze narrowed on him. She slid to the floor next to Lottie, crossing her legs and holding out her plastic teacup. "I'm ready for my second cup," she told the little girl. Then she glanced up at Aaron, who was as stiff-backed as the chair he was seated in. "Relax, Aaron. Take a breath. Felix likes you, see?"

Just as she spoke, Felix removed his fist from his mouth and gave Aaron's cheek a sloppy pat, burbling in baby language as he did so.

"He likes your scruff," Ruby told him. "Which makes sense, seeing as his daddy has a beard."

"Mmm," Aaron answered as Felix repeatedly thumped his chin with his chubby fist, occasionally grabbing his chin hair and giving it a good solid yank.

"Not so hard, now, is it?" Ruby asked him. "Holding a baby is one of life's greatest pleasures. And to think you were missing out on it. Jake is a wise man."

Evidently, she couldn't see his ramrod-straight spine or hear his ragged breathing. This was life's greatest *something*, but Aaron wasn't sure *pleasure* was the right word for it. And he still thought Jake was out of his mind for suggesting the whole thing.

Felix grabbed at Aaron's scruff on both sides of his cheeks and curiously looked him straight in the eyes.

"Look at that. He's taking your measure," Ruby said with a laugh.

Aaron really did feel as if that was what the baby was doing—deciding if he was worthy of this important honor, the distinction of holding such a precious gift straight from God.

Aaron carefully slid his hands around Felix's rib cage and held him up so the baby could see him better. Felix babbled a string of nonsense words and then grinned at him, his four teeth prominent in his smile.

Apparently, he'd passed muster.

Aaron couldn't help but chuckle at the antics of the little imp. Maybe this wasn't so bad after all.

Suddenly, Felix was all arms and legs, squealing and flapping and kicking for all he was worth. His heart hammering, Aaron tightened his hold on the baby and pulled him back into his chest, his breathing labored.

What if he'd accidentally dropped the baby when Felix went all haywire? The poor little guy could have been hurt.

This was *exactly* why he shouldn't be holding a baby at all.

Chapter Eight

Ruby was having the time of her life watching Aaron with Felix. She wasn't at all worried about whether or not he could handle the baby, but she was amused. Here was this marine who'd spent his entire life in total control, suddenly holding a little piece of humanity who scared him to death. Aaron looked as wide-eyed as a deer caught in headlights, although she'd never say so aloud. That was exactly the kind of remark that would send Aaron back into his shell again after she'd worked so hard to coax him out.

Aaron eventually adjusted Felix to a sitting position on his lap, one arm gently circling his waist while he reached for the plastic teacup with his other and took a loud, pretentious sip of "tea."

"Mmm," he said. "Lottie, this tea is super

yummy. Here, Felix, have a taste of your sister's brew. You'll love it."

To Lottie's delight, Aaron held the teacup to Felix's lips and made slurping sounds for him.

"Am I right or am I right? Your sister makes the best tea ever."

Ruby was certain Aaron didn't realize how much his words and actions had delighted the little girl, but it warmed her heart to watch the interaction even so. Aaron was too sweet for words, and he didn't even know it.

Lottie obviously thought so, too. She leaped off the floor and wiggled onto Aaron's knee—the free one not currently taken by her baby brother—and then planted a noisy kiss on the marine's scruffy cheek.

"Thank you, Sarge," she said in the sweetest voice, one that made Ruby's throat close around her breath.

So incredibly precious.

Ruby had seen a whole new side of the tough marine today, from baking cupcakes to tenderly holding a baby in those big, gentle hands of his. She suspected he was likewise recognizing a new way of life that had heretofore been foreign to him.

Did he realize he could move on from here,

maybe have a family of his own to love and protect?

"You're a natural," she said, unable to hold back her smile. "I knew you would be."

He raised a brow. "You think? I have to admit I'm feeling anything but natural right now."

"Felix appears happy to be hanging out with his—*Sarge*. And you totally made Lottie's day."

"I did?" He looked genuinely astonished as his gaze shifted to the little girl, who was now merrily singing to her stuffed animals. "Well, I'll be."

"Given all you've been through today, have you given any more thought to your future?" she gently prodded.

"Every second of every day. It looks pretty bleak from where I'm standing," he admitted, grimacing as if he were in pain.

Maybe he was.

"You're sitting," she teased. "And from where I'm sitting, it looks to me like the possibilities for your future have just opened up wide."

He stared down at Felix, who was noisily sucking on one fist while waving the plastic teacup up and down with the other.

Ruby knew the exact instant when her

words touched his heart. His entire expression changed from the stubbornness he'd carried since the moment he'd arrived in Whispering Pines to one of incredulity and wonder.

And suddenly Ruby understood just what Jake had been after here, forcing him to hold baby Felix. Man to man, without a word, he was showing Aaron a glimpse of what his future could hold if he'd just open up and embrace it.

Aaron glanced up and their gazes met and held. His smile was deep and real and reached out to her in a way she'd never experienced before. For her to be here with him, to be part of something so incredibly lifechanging for the marine who'd thought he'd lost everything, was a blessing beyond any she could have anticipated when she'd first taken on this project.

Yet there was more in his gaze, something to which Ruby didn't dare put a name. His chocolate-colored eyes were full of emotions and a plea for her to help him understand what he was feeling.

But it made her panic and take a mental scramble backward. She'd seen a side of Aaron today that attracted her in ways she couldn't have possibly imagined when the difficult man had first arrived at her facility. A gentler, more tender side of him that rounded him out. He was no longer a cardboard figure of a rough-edged marine who made her want to bang her head against the wall in frustration, but a real three-dimensional man.

And that scared her. Because he was participating in the service-dog program, Aaron depended on her. She was, in a sense, his commanding officer. He needed her guidance if he was ever going to be successful with Oscar—and if she was ever going to nab the military contract that was so important to her own future.

Those were reasons enough for her to stop her wayward thoughts and feelings before they got her into real trouble.

If that weren't enough, she'd seen what combat had done to her father and Daniel. Both had come home different men and had never recovered. True, her father had never asked for or received any help for his problems, and Daniel had only found his way in prison. Aaron was getting help through A New Leash on Love, granted that he had started under duress. She felt he had now accepted what she was offering and was willing to make the necessary changes to make his team with Oscar work.

Ruby sprang to her feet, one palm pressed against her raging heart. Felix had fallen asleep sitting up, the teacup still in his hands, and Lottie was cuddled up on Aaron's shoulder, near napping herself.

"You stay here where you are and enjoy the kiddos," she said, scrambling for an excuse to leave. "I'll take care of the kitchen."

Anything to get away from this situation until she had time to think it through. Her muddled mind was a disaster.

"That won't be necessary," he insisted. "Don't worry about it, Ruby. I made the mess. I ought to be the one to clean it up. I'll get to it later."

"Are you kidding? I had the privilege of eating one of those cupcakes. And I may just steal another one on my way out. Cleaning the kitchen is the least I can do."

Their gazes met again. She could tell Aaron wasn't buying her overly cheerful attitude, but with sleeping kids weighing him down, it wasn't as if he could do anything about it.

She had a way out for now—for which Ruby was eternally grateful.

Though he'd been trying all through the weekend to work it out in his mind, Aaron couldn't understand for the life of him what had happened that had set Ruby off. One second, he and Ruby had been smiling and laughing and sharing time with her sister's kids, and the next she had skittered off as if her life had depended on it.

He didn't know what had happened.

He appreciated what Jake had done for him, forcing him to face his fears and hold baby Felix. He'd come to realize it wasn't about the experience of holding a baby for the first time so much as getting over the mental hurdle that his life post–marine corps would amount to nothing. Holding the baby gave him a glimpse of what might be.

Working with Oscar had taken him a long way as he'd learned to compensate for his injuries. And now, for the first time, he understood that he might indeed have a future— one that included a wife and family. Because he hadn't thought it possible, it wasn't something he'd ever considered, so the realization had hit him over the head like a two-by-four. After he'd enlisted, his only family had been his brothers in arms. It hadn't even occurred to him there might be more to life than living in the past.

He wanted to share that excitement with Ruby. She'd been there for him since the beginning. She'd known him *before*. She'd patiently guided him through the process of learning how to work with Oscar and had shown him there was more to life—that he had a life at all. She'd encouraged him to reach forward and consider what his future might look like.

So, what had spooked her?

Because something certainly had. She'd cleaned up the kitchen—despite him telling her not to—and then she'd dashed off without so much as saying goodbye, which wasn't like Ruby at all.

He was determined to discover the truth as he pulled up to the dog-training facility Monday morning.

"Come on, Oscar. Let's go play." That's what working with Oscar felt like to him now. Not so much of a burden as it was just fun, even with a poodle. Oscar did have his good points, Aaron had to admit, and though he wasn't ready to concede it aloud, he'd really become quite fond of the dog.

Ruby was already outside, working Dandy the black Lab through the agility course, running along with him as he went from obstacle to obstacle. Her cheeks were red from exertion, and several long strands of her hair—which she'd pulled back into a loose bun—had escaped and curled around her face. In his mind, she was more stunningly beautiful when dusty and working than when she was dressed up for church, although she was certainly pretty all the time, no matter what she was doing. But the sparkle in her eyes when she was working with her dogs was second to none.

Aaron let himself and Oscar into the agility arena and watched as Ruby continued to jog from obstacle to obstacle, calling and gesturing for Dandy to correctly perform his tasks. The Lab was young and feisty and didn't always do what Ruby wanted the first time around, but she was patient and simply gestured for him to do the obstacle again and again until he got it right.

This was kind of how she worked with Aaron, he realized. He'd pressed her buttons enough times during the last two weeks to drive anyone crazy, but she'd patiently guided him through every difficulty. Each time he went off course, she'd set him straight, taking him back to the beginning and walking him through the obstacle again. There weren't too many people in the world who could do that.

Major respect.

When Ruby realized Aaron was in the arena watching her, she stopped what she was doing and approached him.

"Sorry, I didn't see you there," she apologized, out of breath, her lungs heaving. "How long have you been watching?"

He grinned. "Long enough. It looks to me as if Dandy needs a little more time and work on the confidence course."

She brushed her hair out of her eyes with the back of her hand. "Yeah, he does. He's still young and spirited, and he doesn't always pay attention when he's going through the—*what* did you call it?"

"Confidence course. That's what they call the obstacle course in the marines. A lot of these obstacles look similar, except we have a forty-foot-drop tower from which every marine has to rappel."

She scrunched her nose and made a face. "Ugh."

He lifted a brow. "Not a fan of heights?"

"Not so much."

He was relieved that they were on speaking terms and she mostly appeared to have gotten over her freak-out moment from Saturday. She'd pretty much ignored him on Sunday at church, so he hadn't been at all certain how today would go. The atmosphere still felt a little stiff between them, though, and he couldn't figure out why. He knew it must have been something he'd said or done, but he hadn't a clue what made this woman's mind work, and most of the time, he wasn't certain he even wanted to know.

"I've got a plastic bin full of two dozen cupcakes for you on the seat," he said, gesturing toward his truck. "Or rather, for the Winslow's Woodlands gift shop. I wasn't sure where you wanted them. Do you want me to drive them down there before we start training today?"

"Wow. Thank you for doing the extra baking this past weekend. Just leave them here for now. Felicity made a spot directly on the front counter of the gift shop to display them, so I'll take them down later. Hopefully, we can keep the boys away from them so our customers will have the opportunity to indulge."

He assumed by *the boys*, she meant her brothers, Sharpe and Frost, both of whom were large men and not boys at all.

"We're keeping this anonymous, right?" he clarified. "Because I really don't want this to get around."

She laughed. "No names will be used. Promise." She crossed her heart with her index finger. "Although in full disclosure, my siblings all know about it. I couldn't keep it a secret from them."

"Good enough. So, what are we doing today?" he asked, changing the subject. "Oscar is quite interested in what you were doing out there with Dandy and is hoping we've come far enough in our training to work the agility course ourselves."

"'Oscar' hopes?" she said, chuckling. "Well, you can tell *Oscar* that running the agility course today is exactly what I have planned for the two of you."

Aaron balked. "*Running* agility?" He couldn't do that if he tried, and he didn't want to make a fool of himself hobbling along, trying to keep up with his dog. He'd watched Ruby and knew he couldn't do what she'd done, but he wanted to push himself.

"Don't worry. He'll do all the running," Ruby assured him.

"I was watching you with Dandy. It seemed to me you were doing at least as much running as he was." He frowned. "How am I supposed to do this?"

Maybe this wasn't such a good idea. He hated—*hated*—his wounds, both the ones people could see and those they couldn't. He'd just been thinking about how trustworthy Ruby was, but at the first sign of a problem, he was ready to bolt back to his truck and take off to anywhere but here, just as he had wanted to do at first.

If he could bolt, which he couldn't.

She propped her hands on her hips. "You're right about that. You won't be able to run the course in the exact same way you just watched me do with Dandy. But—"

He opened his mouth to interrupt her, but she held up a finger to stop him.

"*But* we can make some minor adjustments, and I think both you and Oscar will do fine. It's like with everything else in your life, Aaron. You find another way to do what you want to do."

He hardened his jaw. "Yes, ma'am."

She narrowed her gaze on him. He knew it unsettled her when he called her that. It might have been funny were it not so serious.

She scoffed and shook her head. "Marines. Honestly."

She bent down and scratched Oscar behind the ears. The poodle had been heeling at Aaron's feet since the moment he'd jumped from the cab of the truck. Aaron realized just how far they'd come past the mere basics in two short weeks. He didn't even have to give Oscar commands anymore. The poodle already knew exactly what to do.

"Do you remember how to work an obstacle?" she asked, picking up a clipboard from a small table nearby.

"I think so. I've been studying the course from the notebook you gave me."

"Super. That's good to hear. Let's start with the A-frame again the same way you did before. Up and down, and make sure his paws touch the yellow paint on both sides."

"Okay." He remembered exactly how Oscar had gotten too excited and jumped before hitting the yellow paint the first time they'd tried the obstacle. His heart beat double time as he led Oscar to the A-frame structure and called, *"Hup!"*

Oscar went up and over, his paws touching the yellow paint on the bottom of each side of the obstacle, and then he immediately turned to him, waiting for his next command as to where to go.

"Perfect," Ruby called, marking something on the clipboard. "Let's move over to the slalom."

The slalom, which was a row of evenly spaced poles, was the next obvious obstacle coming off the A-frame, so it didn't take much for Aaron to walk over to it, even without Oscar's assistance. This obstacle, however, looked complicated, although Oscar probably already knew what he was doing even if Aaron didn't. "What do I do?"

"Same as the A-frame. The goal is for Oscar not to miss any of the tight turns. He'll weave right through it."

"Oscar, *hup*," he called, wishing he felt as confident as Ruby sounded.

He shouldn't have been concerned about his dog. He was such a smart pup. Lickety-split, the poodle zipped through the poles, weaving in and out like the expert he was.

"How did you teach him to do that?" he asked in amazement.

"I just put a treat next to his nose and had him follow it as I weaved my hand through the poles. As he became more proficient at it, I lengthened the time between treats until he had the whole obstacle down pat."

Having a fully trained dog made all the difference in the world where the agility course was concerned, although he thought it might be fun to train a dog how to do the training course. They worked obstacle after obstacle one at a time—a full tunnel and a collapsed tunnel, three different standard jumps that looked similar to something used in horse jumping and one hooped jump, the A-frame, the slaloms and a teeter-totter.

Oscar was the master of them all, and

Aaron suddenly found himself oddly proud of his dog, and then even more shocked that he'd so easily segued into that thought—

His dog.

Who knew?

Ruby certainly had. From the very beginning, she'd known. She'd insisted on her choice of Oscar even when he'd balked and squawked about needing a manlier dog by his side. But Oscar was perfect for him. The dog seemed to know exactly what he needed before he even knew he needed it, everything from getting the lights or a bottle of water from the refrigerator to balancing him when he needed a hand—or Oscar's back—to get him to his feet when his wobbly body wasn't cooperating.

Oscar was also a good companion in the evenings and over the weekends. They had even gone on a few hikes now, which was a freeing feeling, especially when he was accompanied by Ruby.

If Oscar had become a friend of sorts, Ruby was doubly so. The best part of his week was the time spent under her tutelage and taking breaks and meals together. He'd never been much of a talker, but Ruby drew him out.

His evenings suddenly felt lonely. Part of it, he supposed, was that he'd spent the majority of his adult life with other marines. There wasn't a lot of privacy during boot camp or on his tours to Afghanistan. Now he was all alone in the evenings, accompanied only by Oscar.

But it was more than that—far more. He was experiencing something brand-new in his life—a real depth of feeling for another human being.

No, not just a human.

A *woman*, with all the craziness that entailed.

He pushed his thoughts and emotions aside, determined not to show weakness even to himself. Maybe that wasn't what it was, but anything out of his control felt like a vulnerability to him, and his feelings for Ruby definitely fell into that category.

"I would like the opportunity to watch you train a new dog or even help you with the process," he said instead of blabbing all the fluffy stuff he was feeling, knowing even as he said the words, he wouldn't be around for any such thing. "I imagine it's quite a challenge, but it also seems like it would be a lot of fun and very fulfilling."

"It's the only thing I've ever wanted to do with my life," she said, sounding thoughtful. "A New Leash on Love started with me, you know. When I was in high school, I rescued a husky from a high-kill shelter in Denver and started training him on a whim. The next thing I knew, my sisters were doing the same thing. One of them fostered a mama shepherd mix and her puppies. Before we knew it, we had a dozen canines and were getting weekly calls from across the state to help rescue dogs. All six of us siblings got together and pitched in to build the facility we have now with the building, the dog run and eventually the agility course."

"What about the service-dog program?" he asked, his curiosity piqued.

"Again, me. I started working with the dogs we brought in to make them easier to adopt out, give them basic training and make them AKC Good Citizen certified. Then I realized I could do additional activities with some of the more gifted pups. We've placed dogs in many situations since then. You've met Lottie's golden retriever, Sissy, who helps her with her epilepsy. My sister Molly's stepson has autism, and we paired him up with a Great Dane named Rufus."

"And now you're helping this poor, pathetic marine."

She narrowed her gaze on him. "Don't talk

about yourself that way. I don't ever want to hear you speak down to yourself again."

"I was just kidding," he assured her, even though that was only half-true. But she'd come out hot, and he didn't want to worry her. Yes, he still felt he was poor and pathetic due to his career-ending injuries, but he found he was dwelling upon that less now ever since coming to A New Leash on Love.

"Anyway, this isn't really about you," she continued.

"Gee, thanks."

She sniffed. "You know what I mean. Your success with Oscar will bring great things to our program. I'm anxious to expand our services with this military contract and help as many veterans as I can."

"Because of your father and Daniel?" He didn't know why he hadn't really put it completely together before now. He was just now truly grasping her vulnerability.

Her eyebrows shot up until they were hidden under her long bangs. "Yes. Partly, at least. But it's more than that now. Since…" She paused and broke eye contact with him. "Well, since meeting you."

His heart leaped into his throat.

Since meeting *him*?

So, it *was* about him, then. Was she telling

him he'd made some sort of a positive difference in her life? Maybe not, but at least he'd had some kind of a good influence on the program, and that was saying something, wasn't it?

For all his brothers and sisters in arms who would enter A New Leash on Love, those who would likewise benefit from this program for which Ruby had worked so hard?

Somehow, he'd forgotten about the endgame here. Along the way, in his mind, it had become about him and Ruby and not about some military contract.

For him.

For her, it was all about getting the contract and always had been.

His gut clenched knowing his part in this would be over in two weeks. But he could do that for her—see that this program was successful with him so it would continue long after he left. He suspected he might be leaving a part of his heart at Winslow's Woodlands when all was said and done.

"Let's conquer this agility course," he said, hoping she couldn't tell he was gritting his teeth against the ache in his chest as he spoke. "What do we need to do next?"

Chapter Nine

❧

Let's conquer the course.

That was all it ever was with Aaron. Coming out the victor. His worldview was all about defeating whatever was in front of him. Ruby wondered what it must be like to feel as if he needed to fight for every last thing.

But then again, he was a marine. Fighting had been his whole life. It shouldn't be so surprising that he thought on those terms.

"I don't want you to run. The ground is uneven in places," she warned him, tapping her pen against the clipboard in her hand as she surveyed the agility course. She'd given quite a bit of thought to how she wanted to do this, but she'd been sidetracked by Aaron.

How easy it was these days for Aaron to affect her and turn her head. After Saturday, watching him with Jake and Avery's children, she'd firmly promised herself that she would avoid thoughts such as these. She had to tamp down her attraction, no matter how strong it was. She'd even gone so far as to avoid him on Sunday at church because her emotions were still in a tizzy and she wasn't certain she wouldn't burst into tears at hello.

She'd pushed herself physically this morning, hoping she could work out her high heart rate and rapid breathing so by the time Aaron came around, she'd be all done with that.

It hadn't worked.

Her heart rate had popped right back up the moment their gazes had locked, and as for her breathing...

"Come around here to the raised platform," she told him. "And then put Oscar up there and command him to sit."

He did as she suggested and waited for further instructions, looking, as usual, as if he was overconcentrating and trying too hard. His eyes were focused on Oscar, and his jaw was so tight Ruby could see his pulse pounding in the corner of it even through his scruff.

"Let's break this down into patterns," she said. "I'd like you to envision three obstacles at a time in the shape of a triangle. What I want you to do is stand in the middle of the triangle of obstacles and guide Oscar from there rather than running by his side through each one. Does that make sense to you?"

"I could try to jog along," he suggested, not quite willing to give up on the idea of some type of normalcy in the run.

"You could, but remember, you don't have Oscar beside you to offer you balance, and the ground is uneven." She shook her head. Aaron probably didn't realize just how much he'd come to depend on Oscar for balance, and she didn't want to have him take a nose-dive just because he was being too stubborn to put his needs first. "Let's just try it my way first. Start with the A-frame and then have Oscar circle around to the collapsed tunnel and send him over the first jump."

Aaron studied the course for a moment and then nodded.

"Oscar, *hup*." He gestured toward the A-frame, and Oscar took off at a dead run. Dragging his foot only slightly, Aaron moved at a fast walk to the middle of the three obstacles, gesturing which way for Oscar to go after he finished one obstacle and moved on to another.

Ruby's idea appeared to be operating quite well. She could tell Aaron had been working hard with Oscar beyond what they did in training every day. The dog never once took his attention away from the marine, and even though there was some distance between them, he was quick to listen to and follow his commands.

Ruby had just known in her heart that the marine and the poodle would make such a great team and had never wavered in her original decision to match Aaron up with Oscar. She smiled as she remembered how adamant he'd been against the pairing. How could she have ever imagined he would put so much effort into making it work between them.

She couldn't be more pleased—or grateful, because she knew he wasn't doing all this hard work for his own benefit. If he'd had his way, he would have left for good before the first training session had even finished.

But he'd stayed—for her.

It wouldn't be long now before his trial would be over. They would be doing a final test at the end of next week, and once he passed that, Aaron would be free to take Oscar and move on with his life, wherever and whatever that may be. The thought caused Ruby's stomach to tighten painfully.

Once she received the contract from Major Kelley, she would have other military men and women coming into the program to follow the same training itinerary Aaron was now doing. She would be ridiculously busy and probably wouldn't have any time to dwell on the past.

Wouldn't she?

Right now, she wasn't so sure. Aaron had taken a place in her life and her heart unlike any client who had come before him. She couldn't imagine the feelings she'd developed for him would simply disappear once he left the program.

No, Aaron would live in her heart long after he left.

"Move to the next three obstacles," she called out, desperately trying to keep her mind on her work. "Teeter-totter, hoop jump and regular jump."

Aaron once again walked to the center of the three obstacles and directed Oscar through with only his voice. Then he moved again to the third set of obstacles and successfully finished the course without a single mistake.

"That worked well," he said after he called Oscar to his side and approached Ruby.

"It did," she said, noting the beading of sweat across his forehead. It was a warm day, but Ruby suspected the dampness on his face was more from exertion than heat from the sun. She was glad she'd forced the issue when it came to Aaron not running the course.

She moved over to a cooler she'd filled with ice and water bottles and handed him a cold one, which he opened up and downed in one long drink. Laughing, she handed him a second bottle. He pressed the bottle to the back of his neck and then sipped more slowly this time.

He appeared frustrated, if the frown on his face and the scowl between his brows were anything to go by. And yet he'd just successfully run Oscar through the entire agility course without a single hitch.

"Are you okay?" she finally asked, knowing Aaron wasn't going to share his thoughts without prompting.

He scoffed and shrugged. "As well as I'll ever be, I guess."

"Meaning?"

"If you knew what I've lived through without giving it a second thought—moving around in heavy tactical gear in 120-degree weather—and now I can barely jog a few feet in jeans and a T-shirt on a mild Colorado summer morning without feeling as if I need to sit down and rest. I can't walk right. I can't breathe right. I'm not even half the man I used to be. It's pathetic."

"No, it's not. And you're not. It just *is*. I know this is difficult for you, but you need to keep fighting."

He grunted in reply and looked away from her.

Now Aaron wasn't the only one who was frustrated. Ruby would have thought after he'd gone so far in the program that he would understand that though his life was going to be altered going forward, that didn't necessarily mean it would be bad.

Just different.

"You have to figure out other ways to do things," she said. "Like with this agility course. You just proved you and Oscar can successfully complete the course if you want to, just in another way than the common path."

He blew out a breath, his gaze dropping to the ground, where he was digging into the grass with the toe of his sneaker.

"Can I try it again?" he asked without looking at her.

"The agility course? Yes. You should," she said. "Only this time, you're going to do the whole course at once rather than in three pieces."

She knew she was pushing him, but that was what he needed right now—to get out of his negative thoughts.

He nodded and finished off his second bottle of water. "Come on, Oscar. Let's show Ruby what we're made of."

He posted Oscar on the platform and then called for him to begin. The run went better than Ruby expected. Oscar was smooth and followed Aaron's lead even though he didn't jog the course with him. The poodle was keen on Aaron's commands.

There was one moment when Aaron stumbled, and Ruby caught her breath, but she laughed when he found his own balance and held up his hand, calling out, "I'm okay!"

Oscar knocked the top PVC pole off one of the jumps, but other than that, he conquered each of the obstacles with ease.

Afterward, with Oscar by his side, Aaron half jogged, half walked back to where Ruby was making notes on her clipboard.

"Better?" he asked. He wasn't grinning with his lips, but Ruby thought she may have glanced a smile in his gaze.

"Much. I'm impressed with you both."

"I know we made a couple of mistakes there. Is it okay with you if I use the course in the evenings? I'd like to practice more before next Friday's big final test."

"It's just pass-fail," she reminded him with a smile. "And I grade on a curve. You've already worked so hard. You don't need to be concerned about how you and Oscar are going to do."

"Maybe not," Aaron said. "But shouldn't I be taking as much of an advantage of this situation as I can while I'm still here?"

His words hit her hard, and she struggled for a moment to regain control over her emotions at the very same time his gaze met hers.

Could he tell what she was feeling?

Hardly, when she could barely decipher herself what those feelings meant.

But that didn't stop her from looking away and busying herself by pretending to make additional notations on her clipboard. Anything so she didn't have to meet his eyes.

She already knew this was going to be the most difficult two weeks of her life. What she didn't know was how she was ever going to get through it, much less successfully get out on the other side.

It just is.

Ruby's words echoed through Aaron's mind for the thousandth time that week and into the next. Whatever he was going to make out of his life moving forward—that was all on him. He could either give up or man up— and for the first time since the explosion had stolen from him what he'd believed was his only role in the world, he was leaning toward the second option.

He was looking for another path forward for his life. He wanted to paint a new picture on his blank canvas.

There were other ways he could contribute to society. According to Ruby and all her siblings, he apparently had mad baking skills thanks to his grandmother, although he still couldn't believe how fast his anonymous cupcakes were moving out of the Winslows' gift shop. Ruby's brothers and sisters, who all knew he was the secret behind the cupcakes, had profusely complimented him on his efforts, one after the other.

So, there was that.

He tried to imagine what being a full-time baker would be like. He could purchase a little shop in town and bake more than just cupcakes—cakes and cookies, perhaps. Spending time in the kitchen was something he enjoyed now that he'd picked it up again, and it did give him a sense of peace he didn't find in much else in his life, but he wasn't certain he could or even wanted to make a career out of it.

Not full-time, anyway.

Dog training came to mind. There was that,

too. As he'd spent the last four weeks inter-acting with Ruby and her dogs, he'd discovered that not only did he have a real knack for working with Oscar, but he also immensely enjoyed the experience and had been spending a great deal of time considering how he might be able to serve his fellow brothers and sisters in arms through working with dogs.

At first it was a general thought, maybe breeding working military dogs—German shepherds and Belgian Malinois—and putting them through basic training before they started their official military careers. But that had its limits. He wasn't physically capable of training a fighting dog. Not with his bad balance. That was beyond him. Anyway, most military dogs were specially bred overseas in Europe.

The more he pondered it, the less viable and interesting that idea sounded.

He had to dig deep to figure out what it was he really wanted, and when the answer finally hit him, his realization almost knocked him over, it was so simple.

And yet so complex.

Lord, I'm gonna need a lot of help with this one.

The truth was, he really wanted to stay here after his time in the program was over. He liked hanging around Winslow's Woodlands and especially A New Leash on Love. He appreciated everything Ruby did with her dogs. He enjoyed living in the mountains, with its fresh air, babbling brooks and backyard hiking trails.

Most of all, he wanted to be here with Ruby, maybe spend more time together to see if there was something real and permanent on which they could build a solid relationship. He already had strong-enough feelings for her that it was something he knew he wanted to pursue.

Whether she felt the same about him was a whole other thing, but he wasn't quite ready to get into that yet, nor was he ready to ask her for a job, as obvious as that next step was. He was ready to do anything in order to work at A New Leash on Love with Ruby, even if all she needed was someone to clean up the dog pens and take care of feeding the canines.

But before he broached his idea with Ruby, he had other stuff to do first, starting with this afternoon. He'd been waiting for the final test since the moment he'd stepped on the Winslows' property, and now that it was Friday and the day had finally come, he needed to keep his mind on his work with Oscar. If he became sidetracked around Ruby, Oscar would pick up on it and they'd make a bumbling mess of the whole test, even if Ruby had assured him it was pass-fail and made it sound as if they were a shoo-in to succeed.

What if he failed?

The fear of failure had been a major hurdle for him throughout his whole life, even as a child, and he supposed it was partly what had made him the man he was. Fear loomed prominently at the back of his mind as he tacked up Oscar and prepared him for the special day. He ran the poodle through a series of basic training exercises to calm both of them down, then hopped in his truck to make his way to the Winslows'.

Ruby was already waiting for him outside, her ginger hair pulled back in a loose bun and a smile on her face. He was used to seeing her with a clipboard tucked under her arm, but this time his eyes were instantly glued to it, as that particular item represented the test itself and was now more than a little intimidating.

She was going to be grading him on that thing, checking off what he'd learned throughout his time in the program.

Pass or fail.

He briefly wondered what would happen if he failed. Would she send him on his merry way, minus Oscar? His heart grew heavy just

thinking about it, and not only because he'd
grown used to having Oscar in his life and
now appreciated all the ways he helped him
in his daily routine.

This was more about Ruby.

But either way, pass or fail, she was going
to boot him to the curb unless he could figure out some clever way around that. Some
reason to stay in town, to stay with her.

Concentrate, he reminded himself. There
would be time for figuring out his future *after*
he passed the course.

"Why don't we move on into the building
and you and Oscar can show me what you've
learned in basic training?"

The corner of Aaron's mouth twitched upward. He knew all about basic training, and
not just of the "sit, down, stay, heel" variety.
And he really wasn't worried about this part
of the test. He and Oscar were on the same
page and had practiced this drill literally hun-
dreds, maybe thousands, of times.

It didn't take them long to work through
all the commands, including putting Oscar
into a *down/stay* and walking clear across
the building to the other side, nearly a football field's length, before calling the poodle
to him. When he sat handsomely at Aaron's

heel and stared up at him with his adoring doggy eyes, he beamed with pride.

Maybe having a poodle wasn't *all* bad.

"That's my good boy," he praised him lavishly. He didn't even have to use food as a motivator for training anymore, but he slipped him a small piece of liver treat anyway and scrubbed behind his ears.

Ruby brought over a folding chair and had Aaron sit in it. "Stand up using Oscar to help you," she commanded, her expression grave. "Really make him work for it, as if you're experiencing a particularly bad day and are having a tough time balancing."

All work and no play for Ruby today, apparently.

Oscar knew the drill. He immediately stood in front of Aaron and tensed his body so Aaron could put his palms on his back and use him to balance as he rose. He didn't move a muscle until Aaron commanded him to heel.

Ruby had Aaron direct Oscar to turn the lights on and off and then retrieve a bottle of water from the refrigerator. If the dog so much as hesitated, Aaron didn't see it. This poodle was astonishing. Props to Ruby for training such an amazing animal.

"Great," Ruby said, writing cryptically on

her clipboard and keeping her scribbling out of his view. Usually, her expression was... if not easy to read, then at least cheery. But right now, her gaze was as serious as the set of her lips. "Okay, we're finished in here. Good job, both of you. Now, we're going to go into town."

"'Into town'?" Aaron echoed, confused. "Why are we going into town?"

She smiled, her eyes finally shining with the light Aaron had been missing all morning. "To finish your test, of course."

"What?" Panic bolted through him like lightning. "I thought we were going to stay around here and do all the outside stuff we've been practicing so hard on. You know—go on a little hike to show off Oscar's balancing prowess and then run the agility course to display his intelligence to finish up."

"Nope. We're going to town. Don't forget, this test is as much about Oscar as it is about you, and what better place to show off his skills than in town?"

Aaron pursed his lips. Wasn't that his whole point? He thought it was much better to display his ability to work with Oscar by hiking and running—okay, walking fast— the agility course. He hadn't anticipated this major hairpin curve in the road, and he felt as if he were going way too fast to be able to turn on a dime, as she was clearly expecting him to do.

She hadn't said a word during this entire training period about having to *go to town* as part of the final exam.

He had believed he'd prepared in every possible way. He'd worked so hard with Oscar every evening, visiting the agility course after hours and even taking small hikes behind the bed-and-breakfast to learn to balance himself over rough terrain with Oscar's help. They'd gone over basic training until there was no question in his mind they would pass.

But going to town?

Not so much.

He felt as if she'd sucker punched him with this new request. He avoided people as much as possible, as Ruby well knew. He went to church, of course, and had visited the grocery store and Sally's Pizza once or twice, but other than that he had avoided Whispering Pines altogether. He always felt people were watching him, although he wasn't self-centered enough not to realize that was probably all in his head. He was so aware of his own awkward movements that he just assumed everyone else saw them, as well.

Wouldn't people wonder why he was dragging his left leg or that he'd have to stop to catch his breath, and why at random moments his expression would turn to one of outright pain?

Oscar had helped a lot with all of that. But that brought up a whole other problem because he would be jaunting around town with a black standard poodle with a teddy bear cut. If people didn't stare at him because of his limp, a man walking around with a froufrou dog was bound to raise some eyebrows and had already the few times he'd visited town.

"What's in town?" he asked suspiciously, trying to sound nonchalant as he placed Oscar in the back seat of the double cab and carefully climbed up into the passenger side of Ruby's truck.

"Your final test," she said, flashing him another smile.

Great. She was actually enjoying this! She finally had her happy demeanor back, and she was using it to torture him.

"I was afraid that's what you were going to say," he admitted. "And yet you never mentioned going to town was a part of our final exam."

She glanced at him, her eyes sparkling. "And yet I didn't."

"So, we're not just picking up feed or anything?"

"Oh, no. We're doing that, too. We may as well make the most of the trip, don't you think? And I always need dog food. I've got a pallet waiting for us at the feed store. But mostly this is for you and Oscar."

"Do I get to know what Oscar and I are supposed to be doing while in town?" He held his breath as he waited for her response. Maybe if he had a list of exactly what she was looking for, he could make sure he and Oscar passed all the points.

"You know in school where you had a test that mostly consisted of multiple choice and true/false questions and then there was a random essay question at the end that was worth most of your grade?"

His shoulders tensed as he nodded. He'd hated high school. The thought of anything academic still gave him hives.

"This is the essay question," she told him.

In other words, this part of the test was open-ended, fly-by-the-seat-of-his-pants. *And* worth most of his grade. His mind scrambled to come up with what Ruby might be expecting, what types of obstacles he might be looking out for, but he was still drawing a blank when they arrived in town and she parked at the back of the feed store.

"Like I said, I've got a pallet of dog food waiting," she told him. "If you can load it up in the back of the truck, that would be great."

He narrowed his gaze on her, trying to second-guess her motives. Loading dog food, he could do, although he had to take only one fifty-pound bag over his right shoulder at a time to make sure he stayed balanced. It used to be he could have easily hoisted two at a time—yet another reminder of how everything had changed. Always on alert, Oscar stayed close to his left heel, ready to step in if he stumbled, which thankfully he didn't do.

Ruby didn't help with the loading. Rather, she kept her eye on Oscar's movements, occasionally scribbling something on her clipboard.

"Okay, now what?" he asked when he had all the bags of dog food loaded in the back of the truck.

"It's a nice day," she told him. "Let's go for a stroll through town."

Chapter Ten

Ruby had to bite the inside of her lip to keep from chuckling when Aaron's face grew pale. It wasn't that she enjoyed torturing him, but this was something he needed to learn, and there was no better time than the present. The poor man was so sure he was the center of everyone's attention any time he went to town that he avoided it like the plague.

It was something she'd never specifically done with any of her other clients because the service dogs had already learned how to be around the people and distractions of town when she and her sisters took them out. But she'd just added it to the syllabus for every service dog–training course. It wasn't until Aaron had come along that she'd realized just how important this objective was.

Aaron was the perfect example of being

too self-aware. He wasn't giving the people of Whispering Pines enough credit. If he had garnered any attention at all, it would be because he was new to town and folks wanted to get to know him—and most of them knew and liked Oscar, although she wasn't sure if he was yet completely comfortable in his skin where the poodle was concerned. He'd certainly come a long way.

New to town and gone tomorrow.

The more she thought about it, the heavier her heart felt. She wished she knew what to say to make things different, but what was there?

His training was over, and he'd performed beyond what she'd ever expected. She remembered the first day they'd met, when she'd been certain this trial would be a complete disaster and utter failure. He had stepped out of the car ready to fight her every step of the way before he'd even known what she or her program offered.

And yet look how it had turned out. He and Oscar were an amazing team. In truth, she'd brought him to town just as much to spend this last little bit of time with him as it was the end of his final test, although she was surreptitiously watching to make sure Oscar's attention remained totally focused on Aaron whenever they passed by people or stopped to speak to someone.

Ruby needn't have bothered. She already knew beyond a doubt that Oscar belonged with Aaron. It was as clear as a sunny day in Colorado.

If only human-to-human relationships were as uncomplicated as canine-human relationships were. It was easy to know what a dog was thinking about you. Even the toughest dogs she'd had, those who'd been abused or neglected, quickly learned to love and trust humans again.

She didn't know if Aaron would ever heal from his wounds and be able to trust and love people again. If she believed he'd made that gigantic emotional step, she'd just open up and tell him what she was feeling, but she suspected all that would do was complicate matters more than they already were.

Ruby understood dogs. Men—one marine in particular—were another thing entirely.

But this wasn't about her. It was about what was best for Aaron, which meant it was better to keep her thoughts and emotions to herself rather than press him on the subject. He was already feeling as if he were in the spotlight as it was.

"There's a lovely little ice-cream parlor at

the end of the street," she said, noticing he was sweating again. She didn't know how much of it was the sun and how much was nerves, but either way, ice cream was always a good idea. "Have you visited it yet?"

He shook his head. "No. I guess I didn't realize it was there, or I probably would have. It's getting hot out here today. Ice cream sounds good right about now."

"I think so, too. What about you, Oscar?"

Oscar wagged his tail and barked once.

"He can have ice cream?" Aaron asked with a surprised laugh.

"Whipped cream or low-fat vanilla soft serve is fine for dogs," she said. "Doug and Kris Little, who own the shop, serve it up special with a dog treat. They know most of our pups since me and my brothers and sisters are regular visitors, and as you know, we've always got a plus-one hanging out with us when we're in town. Oscar is probably already drooling since we're headed that way."

Oscar did, indeed, perk up as they reached the ice-cream shop. Aaron held the door for Ruby and pressed his hand to the small of her back as he entered behind her. She was ultra-aware of his touch and the exact moment he dropped his arm.

"Hey, Ruby. Hey, Oscar," Doug cheerfully

greeted from behind the counter. "And who else do we have with us here today?"

"Doug, this is Sergeant Aaron Jamison," Ruby introduced. "He's in the service-dog training program here with Oscar."

Aaron held out his hand to shake Doug's. "That's a mouthful, and besides, I'm retired from the marines. Just Aaron is fine."

"Aaron, then," agreed Doug. "Thank you for your service, sir. We especially welcome vets here in Whispering Pines. Your ice cream today is on me."

"I—thank you," said Aaron.

"So, you're the well-blessed client who received Oscar as your service dog. Don't tell the other dogs in Ruby's program, but Oscar is my favorite."

"He is?" Aaron asked, sounding somewhat taken aback.

Doug nodded and said, "Yes, sir. He is," and patted Oscar on the head. "What'll you have?" Doug asked.

"For Oscar and me, we'd like the usual," Ruby said, smiling.

"You told me what Oscar likes, but what's the usual for you?" Aaron asked, his expression curious.

"Double-scoop mint chocolate chip in a

waffle cone, with extra whipped cream on top," said Ruby.

Without missing a beat, Aaron said, "I'll have the same."

"Are you sure?" tempted Doug. "We have fifteen kinds to choose from. Granted, not as many as you might find in a larger town, but ours are especially homemade. Everything from the usual to our own unique flavors you won't find anywhere else. Take a peek." He gestured to the glass case.

Aaron took a moment to look over all the offerings and then said, "I'm sure. Mint chocolate chip is my favorite. I would have picked it even if Ruby had other tastes in ice cream."

Hmm. Ruby would have taken him for more of a straight-up chocolate type of guy were she to have guessed, although she had no specific reason why she'd thought as much. To find they had this little thing in common—as ordinary and silly as sharing a favorite flavor of ice cream was—pleased her more than it probably should have.

"One for you," he said, handing Ruby her waffle cone. "One for Aaron, and an exclusive dish for my favorite pooch, Oscar."

"You weren't kidding," Aaron whispered as they slid into a booth, shaking his head as he lifted up Oscar's whipped cream and a doggy treat in a bowl. "He really does have a special treat for the dog."

"And Oscar knows it. Just look how nice he's sitting."

"Yeah. He's staring at me as if he's going to bite my nose if I don't get busy and give him the treat," he said with a chuckle. "Look at those eyes."

He placed the bowl on the ground next to Oscar, and they each settled in and licked at their cones—or whipped cream in a dish with a doggy treat, as the case may be—completely silent for a minute, enjoying the cold ice cream on a warm day and just being together.

"So," Ruby finally said, knowing how desperately she wanted to address this issue but not really wanting to hear the answer, "what are your plans for afterward?"

"You mean after this program is finished—assuming I pass?"

She nodded and reached out her free hand to cover his. "The program is finished, Aaron. There is no question whatsoever that you and Oscar passed with flying colors in every aspect. Even if you aren't quite ready to admit it yet, you and Oscar are a great team, and you belong together."

His gaze widened, but he didn't smile in relief at learning he'd passed the course the way she'd expected him to or even make some under-his-breath comment about how he'd gotten stuck with a froufrou dog.

"That's good… I guess." He didn't quite meet her gaze.

"You guess? What's that supposed to mean?"

"Well, yeah. I mean, I'm glad the test is over. Whew." He made a big production of wiping his forehead with the back of his hand and flinging it to one side as if it had been covered with sweat. "I really, really don't like exams."

"Do you honestly have that bad of test anxiety?"

"You have no idea. There's a reason I joined the marines right out of high school instead of going to college."

"Well, I agree with you there. There are so many more career paths than just college," she said. "I mean, it's good for certain occupations but not necessarily for everything. My brother Frost never liked school, so he took care of the tree farm and our farm animals while Felicity used family savings to get her bachelor's degree in farm and ranch management at Colorado State University. Frost didn't need letters behind his name to be the best man for the job where the animals in our barn are concerned. His trials came through everyday life, and he's succeeded beyond measure. I've never known anyone who cared for animals the way Frost does."

"I thought I'd evaded written tests after the ASVAB—the Armed Services Vocational Aptitude Battery—which I had to take to be recruited in the first place. I studied so hard for that thing and was convinced I wouldn't pass."

"I'm assuming you did, given that you've spent your life in the marine corps."

"I did better than I expected. But I still hate tests."

"At least the final test you took today wasn't in written form," she said, squeezing his hand. "See, it could have been worse."

"It could have been." He smiled at her, and her heart warmed. "I wouldn't say I completely bypassed exams by entering the marines. They had tests of their own, although most of them were practical in nature. There was a written exam that I sweat over the most. I think the only reason I passed was because I was actually interested in all things US Marine Corps, so it was easier for me to study. Still, I'll take ten-mile hikes over written exams any day of the week." He paused. "Well, at least I would have kept up with those long hikes if I'd have been able to stay deployed as I had planned. That's kind of out of the question now, isn't it?"

"You've had more than your share of trials lately, physical and otherwise," she agreed. "And only one has been formal. I don't even think the worst of it is what the world expects of you. You put far too much pressure on yourself."

His gaze widened. "I never thought about it that way."

"You should. And although you have a lot to look forward to in your future, I believe you should look back at the four weeks we've had together and realize how far you've come." Her throat closed around the last words, and she had to fight to keep her emotions steady.

His jaw tightened and he shook his head. "I don't want to look back anymore. I've spent far too much time doing that, and there's no good to be had in it. Instead, I need to look forward and see what's right in front of me and what's to come."

"That's healthy. What do you see?" she asked, genuinely curious. "Do you have an idea in mind for what your immediate future looks like?"

He regarded her for a moment before nodding. "I might."

"That sounds cryptic."

He curled up one side of his lips. "I don't really want to talk about it yet, at least not until it's more of a sure thing."

"I see." She stared at him for a long time, but he didn't elaborate.

She didn't see, but she wished she did. After tomorrow, whatever he planned for his new life would be his own business, and he didn't appear to want to share it with her. She probably wouldn't even know what happened to him after he left, and that saddened her on many levels.

"But I'll let you know as soon as I know," he assured her.

She jumped in before she could talk herself out of it. "Although we never ended up using it, we exchanged phone numbers at the beginning of the program so I could get a hold of you if I needed to and vice versa. Would it be okay if I held on to your number and touched base with you from time to time?"

"Well, sure," he agreed. "I'd like that."

"Just to see how you and Oscar are progressing and to make sure there aren't any new issues," she added and then wanted to stuff a sock in her mouth. Why couldn't she just have left her question without the qualifier?

The smile dropped from his face. "Right.

Of course, you'll want to check up on me and Oscar."

Somehow, she got the feeling that response wasn't exactly what he'd been expecting. And if that wasn't it, then...*what*?

Butterflies let loose in her stomach.

"Our graduation ceremony isn't what you'd typically find at the end of a program," she told him, changing subjects before her emotions got away from her. "No 'Pomp and Circumstance,' no parading across a platform in front of everyone to receive your diploma."

"Thankfully," he muttered under his breath before taking a large bite out of his cone.

She smothered a giggle, knowing how painful even thinking of such a situation would be for him. "We're having a bonfire on our property this evening," she said. "Don't worry. It's just my family, but we'd all like to celebrate your accomplishments with you. And you do get an official certificate of completion, even without all the hype."

He just stared at her for a moment, and who could blame him? With Ruby, *just family* wasn't exactly a small gathering of people. But she thought he was fairly comfortable with all her brothers and sisters and their families, as he'd spent a lot of time around them, especially Jake and Avery.

"It's really casual," she assured him. "My brother Frost may bring his guitar, and then we'll sit around the fire, roasting marshmallows and singing. Super relaxed."

"I don't sing," he said, his voice extra raspy.

She chuckled. "Oh, no. I didn't expect you to sing. Not unless you want to. Oscar has a nice voice, though."

On cue, Oscar howled a few notes.

"Shh," Aaron said, pulling his hand out from under Ruby's and pressing his palm over Oscar's muzzle. "We're in a restaurant, you silly dog."

"It's an ice-cream shop. And I can guarantee you Doug doesn't mind a little extra doggy noise."

"*I* mind." His voice squeaked.

She laughed. "Breathe, Aaron. You need to relax. The worst part—your final test—is over."

"Does that mean we get to go home now?"

Home?

What kind of a slip of the tongue was that?

Or had he meant anything by it at all?

Had he been referencing the bed-and-breakfast? Or was it A New Leash on Love he considered his home? She wished she could just ask him. Or invite him to stay in town awhile while she figured out exactly what she was feeling.

Or...*something*.

But she suddenly became just as tongue-tied as Aaron usually was. Her heart was there but the words were not. And even if they had been, would it really be fair to Aaron to be bringing this up on the day before he was supposed to leave?

What was she going to say? Oh, and by the way, even though you already have future plans, I think I may have feelings for you. Do you want to stay in Whispering Pines for a while so I can figure out my emotions?

Awkward.

Awkward and unfair.

That would be putting undue pressure on him. No. That would never do. She wouldn't put him in that kind of position, no matter how hard it was on her heart.

This was something she'd have to deal with on her own.

Aaron squirted gel onto his palm and rubbed his hand through his dark hair, trying to make it look presentable. He'd never worried overmuch about his appearance, but tonight it felt important for him to look his best—and it wasn't because he was going to receive a certificate of completion tonight.

No, this was for a completely different, pretty redheaded reason.

Despite Ruby having said the evening was casual, he was wearing his best black jeans, and he'd bought a new long-sleeved black button-down shirt for the occasion.

"What do you think, Oscar?" he asked the dog, who was stretched out on the floor in front of the bathroom door. He held his arms out and turned around in a circle. "Do I pass muster?"

He was completely over feeling strange about keeping up a running conversation with his dog. He was so used to it now he couldn't even remember what it had been like before Oscar was part of his life. He couldn't believe he'd thrown such a fit about it at first.

Jake had caught him a time or two yapping to Oscar about one thing or another and razzed him about it, but he knew how important Jake's own dog, Sissy, was to the Cutter family. It was all in good fun. Everything the gregarious Texan did was all in good fun. He'd married into the Winslow family and had found his place in the world, and the man was as happy as the proverbial lark.

Sang like one, too.

Knowing he was tone-deaf, Aaron had no intention of singing a single note this evening, but he planned to thoroughly enjoy this last night with the Winslow clan—especially his time with Ruby.

He'd been thinking about what he'd say to her, how he would approach his ideas and the suggestion that perhaps he could stay around, maybe help her out in some way, as Jake did with Avery. If only he was better with words. Even if he wrote everything down and read it off a piece of paper, he would probably garble the whole thing when it came time to speak.

Actions spoke louder than words anyway. Maybe it would be better for him to hold off on speaking about his intentions until he'd actually gone and done what he envisioned doing—the first half of his plans, at least, so he could come to her with something tangible to offer instead of just an idea.

Then when he approached Ruby, he could do so without putting any pressure on her to make a decision based on the financial condition of the service-dog program, since he didn't know where A New Leash on Love stood in that regard. He wanted Ruby to know his idea was workable whether she was looking for help in training her dogs or not. He'd even be willing to work for free, assuming everything else went according to plan. This wasn't about money, or even what position she might or might not offer him when he asked.

Tonight, he decided as he put a newly bathed Oscar in his truck and slid in beside him in the growing darkness, he would try to concentrate on simply enjoying time with Ruby and her family at the bonfire. If he could ingratiate himself to them the way Jake and Logan, who'd married Ruby's sister Molly, had done, all the better.

When he pulled his truck into the lot at Winslow's Woodlands and turned off his headlights, he had a good laugh at himself for all the trouble he'd gone through. There was no moon tonight, and he hadn't thought to bring a flashlight, so the only way Ruby would be able to see him would be through the light of the bonfire.

And he'd bought a new shirt for this.

The whole Winslow clan, along with their families, were already at the bonfire when Aaron approached, but Ruby was the first to see him, and he couldn't help but think she'd been watching for him, especially when she ran up to him and curled her arm through his, dragging him toward the bonfire.

"You look extra handsome tonight," she

told him with a smile that was even more animated than usual.

Extra handsome?

He wouldn't have even put himself in the *regularly* handsome category on his best day.

"That's only because it's pitch-dark and you can't see anything other than my shadow," he told her with a chuckle.

She moved closer to him, rubbing a hand across his shoulder and briefly around his neck.

"New shirt?" she murmured, her voice so soft it made his gut turn over.

Now, how would she know that when she was flying blind?

"Yes, but before you start thinking I ran out to one of the clothing stores in Whispering Pines to purchase something decent for tonight... I totally did," he finished, his voice trailing off.

She threw her head back and laughed. "And you forgot to take off the tag."

He groaned and swiped a hand down his face, feeling it heat under his palm. He was suddenly glad it was so dark in the woods.

"Here—lean down a sec and I'll get it for you." She stood on tiptoe, and with one quick jerk of her hand, she snapped the little string of plastic that held the price tag.

"There," she said cheerfully, handing him the tag without looking at it. "Now how much you shelled out for your clothes will remain a mystery."

He couldn't help but smile at the way she was insinuating he'd ever step foot into a high-end clothing store—although of course, though he wouldn't admit it to her, the whole reason he'd gone to all the trouble of buying a new shirt at all was just to impress Ruby.

"Like I said, I got it here in town," he said, feeling silly that they were still discussing his shirt. "I didn't tap into my pension."

She laughed again and held out her hand to him, taking his hand in hers and linking their fingers, making his heart warm. "Come on. All the others are waiting for us at the bonfire. Let the celebration begin!"

He'd momentarily forgotten he was supposed to be the center of attention tonight. In effect, this was his graduation ceremony, however casual Ruby had promised it would be.

Breathe, he coaxed himself when everyone's eyes turned upon him. *Ruby would tell you to relax. You know everyone here.*

And he did—some only slightly and others with whom he'd spent a lot of time, like Jake and Avery, and Felicity in the gift shop, where he still couldn't provide enough cupcakes to keep up with the demand for them even though he was now delivering them three times a week on Mondays, Wednesdays and Fridays.

He wished he weren't so self-conscious all the time, like tonight, when everyone would be rooting for him. He knew it drove Ruby crazy when he pulled into himself. Before his accident, he never used to be that way. He'd led men into battle with all the confidence in the world. And now it was hard for him to calm down enough to take part in a friendly family gathering?

The bonfire was already carefully and safely built and raging. It looked as if this was something they did fairly regularly, for there was a firepit in a clearing, and they had placed large tree trunks in a circle around the bonfire. Some people were sitting atop the logs, while others were settled on the ground, using the logs as a backrest.

When they reached the bonfire, Ruby sat first, flopping down on the earth with her legs crossed and patting the ground beside her, which was mostly dirt with an occasional swatch of grass covered with green pine needles. He slid down next to her, expecting it to be awkward and possibly a little bit painful, but it was more comfortable than he'd imagined it would be. The pine needles may have looked poky, but instead they felt more like a soft blanket underneath him. He leaned his back against the log and stretched out his arms. Oscar flopped down at his feet and immediately rolled in the dirt. So much for bathing him. Good thing he was dark-colored to hide the dirt.

"This is one of my favorite things to do," Ruby said with a contented sigh as she curled under his arm and leaned into his chest. "I'm so busy with work that I don't take too many nights off, but when I do, I want to do something relaxing and fulfilling, something that will fill my creative well, you know?"

"Mmm." He wasn't even certain he had a creative well, and he was still feeling a bit nervous about the evening, but he wasn't going to admit that to Ruby. She looked as relaxed as he wished he could be. He wouldn't take that away from her.

The fire snapped, crackled and popped worthy of a bowl of rice cereal, and its glow left Ruby looking beautiful beyond words. Aaron choked up as he watched her close her eyes and lean her head back on his shoulder.

As Ruby had predicted, before much time had passed, Frost drew out his guitar. At first, he strummed a couple of tunes and everyone just listened, but then he played a song everyone recognized, and Jake jumped in, his full bass lighting up the night with sound. Soon, nearly everyone had joined in, even Ruby with her silky soprano. The only one not singing was Aaron. His voice was too raspy, and he couldn't carry a tune, so he wouldn't torture anyone here by attempting to sing.

No one appeared to notice that he hadn't joined them, and soon he'd forgotten how uncomfortable it made him. He was enjoying everyone else's combined voices, complete with beautiful harmonies. The six siblings had clearly grown up singing together, and their voices blended very well.

He closed his eyes and inhaled the sweet citrus scent of Ruby's shampoo. This night could not be any better.

"Time for s'mores," Frost said at last, setting aside his guitar for the time being. "Sharpe has the sticks. Who was in charge of bringing the marshmallows this time around?"

"That would be me," said Felicity, patting a nearby icebox. "Marshmallows, graham crackers and chocolate bars. We're good to go."

Felicity passed out the goodies, and Sharpe handed each of them a long, green branch on which to spear the marshmallows. Soon, many of Ruby's siblings had a marshmallow hovering close to the fire.

Aaron had heard of toasting marshmallows and eating s'mores, but this was his very first time actually participating. It wasn't something he'd ever had the opportunity to do as a child. The only camping he'd ever done was in the military, and he was looking forward to his first taste of this special treat.

"How do you like your marshmallows?" Ruby asked him with a soft smile. "Light brown or black and burned to a crisp?"

"'Burned'?" he asked, curling his lips down. "Why would anyone intentionally burn their marshmallow?"

"Crisp on the outside, gooey on the inside," she informed him. "Don't knock it unless you've tried it."

"I'm pretty sure I would never do that on purpose," he said. "But to be honest with you, I've never roasted marshmallows before. I lived in a big city growing up."

"Oh, my. Then you really don't know what you've been missing. Be prepared to be amazed."

She fitted her marshmallow onto the sharp end of her branch. Aaron watched her before doing the same, and then they both put their marshmallows over the fire to roast.

True to her word, Ruby dropped her stick deeper into the flame, and her marshmallow quickly blackened to a crisp. Aaron kept his well above the fire and pulled it out when it had barely turned a light brown.

They made their s'mores, stacking the bars of chocolate and their marshmallows between squares of graham crackers. Ruby took a bite and squealed in delight.

"Oh, this is so good. I need to do this more often."

Aaron wrinkled his nose. It seemed to Aaron like it was a lot of effort to go through just for a crumbly, sticky mess, but he stacked up his s'more and took a bite for Ruby's sake.

To his surprise, it was delicious. It was also just as sticky and crumbly as he'd imagined it would be, so he kept taking quick bites, sharing an occasional bit of graham cracker with Oscar until he'd finished it.

"See? What did I tell you?" Ruby teased. "Tell me that wasn't the best dessert you've ever had—well, maybe not the very best. Your cupcakes have earned that honor."

"You're right. It was good," Aaron admitted, licking marshmallow from his fingers. As good as the s'more had been, he didn't really want to go around for the rest of the evening with sticky fingers.

Thankfully, at that moment Felicity thoughtfully came by with antibacterial wipes, and he was able to get his hands clean.

When Frost picked up his guitar again and resumed his strumming, Ruby rolled to her feet and held a palm out for him to stop.

"Before we get back into the singing," she said, "I would like to take a moment to commend Aaron for a job well done in the service-dog program and present him and Oscar with their certificate of completion. Aaron, would you stand and come over here beside me, please?"

He'd rather not, but he'd anticipated this part of the evening, so he used Oscar to help him stand and balance before he moved to Ruby's side, brushing the dust off his jeans as he went.

"When Aaron first came here to participate in the program," Ruby said, tears shining in her eyes, "I have to admit I didn't have high hopes for this to work. Aaron had a lot to overcome. But he's such a brave man, and with Oscar's help, he has come farther than I could even have imagined. I'm proud this evening to present him and Oscar with his certificate of completion. Aaron, Oscar is now officially your service dog. Congratulations."

"Thank you," he said, then cleared his throat. His voice was so raspy and low he could barely speak. He had something important he wanted to say, but he wasn't sure he could get the words out.

The Winslow siblings applauded him and held up their water bottles to toast him. Jake whooped and whistled.

He waited until the noise had died down before trying to speak again.

"I just want to say a few words about this program—and most specifically about Ruby, and what they mean to me. You already know what a special, beautiful person she is both inside and out. When I first came to A New Leash on Love, I didn't believe she could help me—especially after she introduced me to Oscar."

When he said Oscar's name, he barked, and everyone laughed.

"And believe me, Aaron told me so," Ruby said. "His froufrou dog."

"To tell the truth, I didn't trust her, especially where choosing me a dog was concerned. I didn't understand at all where she was coming from. And I figured if she didn't get that part right, how would she possibly be able to train me?" He shook his head. "I don't have to tell you how wrong I was. She was one brave woman, standing her ground with Oscar and a stubborn marine. Ruby, I just want to thank you for not giving up on me when you had every reason to."

She reached out and squeezed his hand. "Likewise. You gritted your teeth and kept on going even when I know you didn't want to. You never quit."

Again, her siblings offered major applause and a hoot or two as Ruby handed Aaron his certificate.

When she smiled up at him, he got all choked up. He wasn't usually a man who experienced deep emotions, but he was definitely feeling overwhelmed now.

"I—thank you," he stammered. "I appreciate everyone's support. Let me put this away in my truck before it gets dusty."

Then he made a figurative run for it, Oscar at his heel—away from people and out of the light.

Chapter Eleven

Ruby joined her brothers and sisters in singing a few hymns and praise songs they knew from church. They'd been singing in harmony since they were little kids, and it was something Ruby especially enjoyed. Since she was a second soprano, she got to sing the melody, so it wasn't hard for her to keep pace with them. She let her other siblings do the hard work—Felicity's soaring first soprano, Molly's vibrant contralto, Avery's rich first alto, Sharpe's smooth tenor, Frost's lush baritone. Jake's deep voice joining in the bass and Molly's husband, Logan, singing first tenor. It was almost as if God had put them together as their very own choir, and Ruby appreciated these special moments with her family.

Fifteen minutes later, when Aaron still hadn't returned to the bonfire, she began to worry. She knew he didn't like to be up in front of people because he was self-conscious about his wounds.

Had this been too much for him?

She hoped he hadn't ducked and ran. This was their last night together, and Ruby didn't want to miss a moment of it, so she excused herself and went to find him. The first place she checked was where he'd parked his truck, since he'd mentioned taking his certificate back there. She breathed a sigh of relief to find the vehicle right where he'd parked it earlier.

But he wasn't anywhere to be found. Reaching his truck, she focused her flashlight beam on the front seat of his cab. His certificate of achievement was on the passenger seat, so he had been by to drop it there and couldn't be far off.

"Aaron?" she called into the dark night air and listened closely, but she didn't receive any kind of response. She followed her call with, "Oscar?" thinking the dog might bark.

It didn't happen, so Ruby picked her way back toward the bonfire, staying just out of the firelight so she wouldn't be seen by her family as she started a perimeter inside the forest. Feeling Aaron might be seeking time alone to regather his composure, she flicked off her flashlight so she wouldn't draw any attention to herself or him. She could barely see her feet through the flicker of the bonfire into the tree line, but she'd spent her whole life on this land and was as sure-footed as a goat— something she knew because their farm actually *had* goats, and she'd seen firsthand all the antics of which they were capable.

"Aaron?" she whispered again into the darkness.

She heard the rustle of pine brush and turned in that direction.

"Aaron?"

"Over here," she heard after a minute more of walking. The firelight barely came through now, no more than the slightest glimmer, but her eyes managed to make out the silhouette of broad-shouldered Aaron standing beneath a lodgepole pine, leaning his back against the trunk with his hands stuffed in the front pockets of his jeans.

She approached him, near enough that she could feel his warm breath on her cheek. She could barely make out his gaze, so she reached for his hand.

"Feeling overwhelmed?" she whispered tenderly.

He shook his head. "No. I just needed a minute to absorb everything."

"I'm sorry. I should have known you wouldn't want any kind of public ceremony, even if it was just here with my brothers and sisters."

"It's not that. I've gotten to know them over the past four weeks, and I'm aware they want the best for me. That isn't what drove me away."

"What is it, then?"

"You know I'm not used to speaking in front of people—not unless I'm barking out orders, which I don't do anymore."

She remained silent until he had pulled himself together enough to continue.

"I started talking and I got all choked up with emotion," he admitted. "I couldn't believe it myself to find tears were burning in the back of my eyes. That's never happened to me before. I've never cried in my life."

"There's nothing wrong with tears, you know. You're a human being. You're allowed to have feelings now and again."

"No. I know. That's just not who I am."

"And it scared you?"

"Not exactly. It definitely made me feel uncomfortable. And I knew if I stayed around any longer, it might frighten me out of my gourd. So, I took the easy way out and bolted, which appears to be my new MO."

Speaking of emotions, her heart welled up with feelings for this quiet marine. She knew he'd probably never feel natural when he was experiencing strong emotions, but she was glad he'd trusted her enough to share this moment with her.

"So, you are off tomorrow, then," she said softly, struggling to keep her own emotions from bubbling out. He was already on the verge of running. If she started bawling, the poor man would head for the hills for sure.

"I am," he agreed without missing a beat.

She was surprised when he smiled. It was like a stake in her heart. *She* wasn't happy about him leaving, but he evidently couldn't wait to get away.

"I know you and Oscar will be successful wherever you land," she said, despite her own feelings on the matter.

"You know, I think we will," he agreed. "I really think we will."

His voice had grown increasingly raspy, and she wondered if perhaps he was feeling a little of the same emotions she was.

Their gazes met and locked, and though she could only see him through the faintest flickers of firelight, she nearly drowned in the chocolate depths of his eyes. She wanted to stay there and never come out again, and so she did the most natural thing in the world for her to do.

She reached up and held his face between her hands, his soft scruff scratching her palms as she pulled his head down to hers.

Closing her eyes, she put every emotion she was feeling into her kiss. This was the only place in the world she wanted to be—now, and maybe always.

But then he leaned back, tilting his head as he looked at her.

"What are we—" he started to ask in a low, husky tone, his eyes glittering in the firelight.

In a panic, Ruby tried to pull away. She'd obviously just made a terrible mistake and had completely misread the situation.

But in a single moment, Aaron had taken control, wrapping his arm around her waist and turning her around so it was her back against the trunk of the tree. He framed her face in one large hand and braced himself against the tree with the other, and then his lips were on hers again.

Sweet yet strong. Both giving and taking. Saying far more without words than he ever had spoken aloud.

She didn't know what the future held, but this felt good.

Right.

And then he pushed away from her. He grabbed both of her hands in his and took two steps backward, kissing the back of each hand before dropping them and disappearing into the dark of the forest, Oscar at his heel.

She knew in her heart he wouldn't be coming back to the bonfire.

And she couldn't imagine anything worse.

For she now finally understood just how smitten she was.

And he was gone.

The Saturday-morning sun shone through the curtains at the Winslows' bed-and-breakfast, raising Aaron from the best night's sleep he'd had in—well, maybe ever.

No bad dreams. No night terrors. No waking up in a cold sweat.

Just the memory of Ruby. Oh, how he'd welcomed her expression of emotions. It made what he was doing today mean all that much more.

The moment their lips had met, Aaron had known for sure his feelings were genuine. He couldn't wait to start the day and see where it would take him.

Hopefully back to the Winslows so he could share his thoughts, plans and dreams with Ruby.

But first he had a full day planned.

He gave a very dusty Oscar another bath and blow-dried his hair. If someone would have told him a year ago, he would even own a blow-dryer, much less that he would use it on his dog, he would have laughed right in their face. Now it was just a regular part of his routine, and since Oscar always accompanied him wherever he went, he felt it was important that the poodle be in fighting shape today.

While Oscar waited, Aaron showered and trimmed up the week's growth of beard on his face. His gut was churning with nerves. A lot rested on the results of today's mission.

Oh, who was he kidding?

Everything rested on whether or not he succeeded today.

"Come on, boy," he said, calling Oscar to his side. "Let's win over some townspeople today."

He drove into Whispering Pines with his heart in his throat. He'd never had to sell anything before, and in a way, he was selling himself as much as his product. Would anyone buy the idea of a baking marine?

His first stop was Sally's Pizza. At least he knew Sally, so this wouldn't be quite so hard. Thankfully, Sally was there and came out of the kitchen to greet him the moment he walked in the door of her restaurant. He carried a picnic basket with a tub of fresh-baked cupcakes under one arm. He'd originally intended to create some sort of flyer to advertise his wares but then decided the best way to sell cupcakes was to pass them out for everyone to taste.

"Well, if it isn't Aaron and Oscar. It's good to see you again. Where's the pretty redhead who usually accompanies you?"

"I just graduated from the service-dog program last night, and I'm on my own today," he told her, feeling awkward about sharing his accomplishment.

"Congratulations!" Sally said loud enough for every customer in her restaurant to turn and see what all the fuss was about. "This young man just graduated from Ruby Winslow's service-dog program," she announced merrily. "Can we get a big round of applause for him and Oscar?"

Aaron felt the heat rise to his face and knew his cheeks had to be the color of a ripe tomato. If only Sally knew how incredibly painful it was for him when people drew attention to him.

"Can I have a moment of your time, Sally?"

he asked, trying to get to the point of his visit. "I won't take too long."

"Are you ordering?" She lifted one brow.

He chuckled. "I'll take a slice of your famous pizza if you promise to sit down in a booth with me for a second. I have a proposition for you."

"Sounds intriguing. You want everything except anchovies?"

"You remember."

"Of course, I remember one of my favorite customer's favorite pizza toppings," she teased. "What do you take me for? Give me one second and I'll be right back out with your pizza."

Aaron slid into a booth near the back, placing the basket of baked goods next to him. Oscar pressed his head against Aaron's thigh, and he absently scratched behind his ears.

"You can tell I'm nervous, can't you, boy?" he whispered. He was no longer overly concerned that someone might be watching him or that he was speaking to his dog, even in a public place. All of that seemed normal to him now.

Sally reappeared with an extra-large slice of pizza and a glass of water and sat down opposite him. "Now, then. Tell me what I can do for you today."

Aaron folded his hands on the tabletop and smiled at Sally. "As you know, I just finished my service-dog training, and technically my string to A New Leash on Love has been cut."

"Uh-huh," she said, nodding. "But…?"

"But I've come to appreciate what Whispering Pines in general—and Winslow's Woodlands in particular—has to offer. The truth is, I'd like to stick around, if that's possible."

Her eyebrows rose. "You looking for a job delivering pizzas? It's not much of an hourly wage, but you're cute enough that you'll get good tips from ladies young and old alike."

He threw his head back and laughed, something he hadn't done much of in his life, and he didn't even care when people curiously glanced in his direction.

"While I appreciate the job offer, I'm actually here to offer something to you, if you're interested. Have you been up to the Winslows' lately?"

She shook her head. "Can't say that I have."

"Well, long story short, a couple of weeks ago, Ruby caught me baking my grandmother's cupcakes at the bed-and-breakfast, and she convinced me that I ought to put some up for sale at the gift shop. I agreed under duress, and only because they kept it anonymous. I have to say I was surprised at first that Felicity couldn't seem to keep them in stock."

Sally's eyes lit up with interest. "Let me get this right. You're a handsome marine who also bakes. Please tell me you're offering me cupcakes."

He smiled. "I am. In fact, I've brought a sample for you today. If you like what you taste, I'm hoping to be able to make a side-hustle business out of it. I can deliver three times a week on Monday, Wednesday and Friday afternoons."

He realized he was getting ahead of himself and backed off, took a deep breath and reached for a cupcake from the tub inside the basket.

He handed it to her and watched as she nibbled away at it, taking tiny, birdlike bites and murmuring unintelligible words after each one. Aaron was sweating by the time she'd finished the whole cupcake, and still she didn't speak.

"Well?" he finally asked, unable to wait a moment longer. "Tell me what you think. Did you like it?"

She shook her head and dabbed at her mouth with a napkin before speaking. "No. Definitely not."

Aaron's heart, which had been lodged securely in his throat and pumping a mile a minute, dropped like a stone to his stomach.

"No?" he echoed, taking a bite of pizza to keep his disappointment from showing up in his expression.

So much for his brilliant idea.

"No," she repeated. "I *loved* it. I've never tasted anything like it, bar none. Aaron, you're an absolute genius."

His mouth was dry, and he couldn't seem to swallow his bite of pizza, so he took a long drink of water before responding. "No, actually, my grandmother is the genius here. It's all on her. I just followed her recipe."

"From one chef to another, I think we both know what utter bunk that is. Anyone can follow a recipe, but not everyone has such spectacular results when they do."

He was blushing again. "Thank you, ma'am. I appreciate it."

"How much per dozen?" she asked.

He'd been going over figures in his head since he'd first come up with the idea but wasn't sure what number to put out there. He had to recoup what he spent in baking materials and needed to make some sort of profit, but he didn't know what would be fair to the townspeople. Felicity was selling them for three dollars each, but that was out of the

Winslows' unique gift shop, and he thought she might be getting a little more out of it than it was worth for that reason.

"Honestly, I'm not sure," he admitted. "That's why I stopped here first before I spoke to anyone else. I trust you and figured you'd be straight with me. What do you think is a good price?"

"Honey, I can sell these things for three bucks a pop easy. That's thirty-six dollars for a dozen. Let's say an even twenty-five dollars. Fair enough?"

"More than fair," Aaron said, his heart beating rapidly. This might actually work. "And how many dozen would you like?"

"These are going to fly out of my restaurant. Let's start with three dozen three times a week, and we'll probably have to go up from there."

Aaron wanted to pump his fist but barely restrained himself from doing so. Oscar picked up on his energy and barked animatedly.

"I see Oscar is excited about your new endeavor, as well."

"He's my partner in crime. I suspect he'd like to stay in town, where he can see Ruby from time to time, as well," he said, patting Oscar to calm the poodle down—or to calm himself down, depending on how he was looking at it.

"Oh... I see," Sally said with a giggle. The woman might be creeping up in years, but she pulled off her giggle as well as a girl in the middle of a high school crush.

"I'm sorry?" he asked. "See what?" He wasn't following her.

"It's quite clear to me now that it's *Oscar* who wants to stay in town and see Ruby from time to time," she said with a knowing smirk.

He choked on his last bite of pizza as heat flooded his face, his ears burning as hot as Ruby's blackened marshmallow. At first, he started to deny her accusation—if he could call it that—but then he stopped himself before the words left his mouth. After all, he really *was* staying in town for Ruby's sake. If she told him she had zero interest in pursuing a relationship, he wouldn't have any inclination to stick around.

His mind briefly flitted to their kiss. He had to believe in those emotions, or he was wasting his time here.

"Ruby's caught your attention, has she?"

He looked Sally straight in the eye when he answered, "Yes, ma'am."

"Good on you. Ruby deserves some true happiness in her life. I've been telling her that for quite some time, but I now see she was waiting for God's best for her. You take care of her, you hear?"

God's best?

Was that what he was? He'd never been that for anyone before.

"Yes, ma'am," he told her when he realized she'd narrowed her gaze on him.

"I won't have to threaten to take you down if you don't care for her as she deserves. Not with Sharpe and Frost around."

"No kidding," Aaron muttered. "I wouldn't mess with those two. But I promise you, Ruby is first and foremost on my mind."

Sally reached out and made an *X* on his chest. "And in your heart."

"Yes, ma'am."

He tried to pay for his pizza, but Sally would have none of it. "Enjoy your day," she told him. "I wish every blessing on you and Ruby."

He could only hope the rest of his day went half as well as his time with Sally had. His next stop was the ice-cream shop. Doug Little was behind the counter and reached out his hand as soon as Aaron walked in.

"What can I do for you today?" he asked, coming around to pet Oscar. "No Ruby with you today?"

Funny that everyone in town expected Ruby to be by his side. It was his deepest prayer that Ruby wanted the same thing.

"Ruby doesn't know about this yet," he explained, as he had to Sally. "I'm looking to start a side hustle in order to stay in town. I intend to bake cupcakes to sell in Whispering Pines, and I'm here trying to find out if it might be feasible to sell them here in your shop, if you'd have any interest in that?"

"Cupcakes and ice cream? Seems to me those go together."

"Here you go, sir," Aaron said, handing him a cupcake from the basket. "Try before you buy."

Doug ate the cupcake in silence, but unlike with Sally, Aaron could immediately tell he liked it. He was grinning from the first bite.

"Chocolate is my favorite," Doug said, wiping white frosting from his lips with the corner of his apron. "How much are you selling these for?"

"Sally at the pizza joint said she could easily sell them for three dollars apiece, which comes to thirty-six dollars a dozen. She suggested I ask for twenty-five dollars of that."

"That sounds more than reasonable. I can tell these will fly off the shelf."

Aaron went over the delivery schedule and

how many dozens Doug would need, and before he knew it, he was out on the street again. He'd originally planned to hit up more shops, but between Sally and Doug—and presumably the Winslows, once they knew he was staying in town—he already had more than enough for his part-time business.

If he had to, he could increase his baking and make it a full-time business, perhaps reaching out to neighboring towns if necessary or setting up a shop in Whispering Pines. But first he wanted—no, *needed*—to see if Ruby would be interested in having him help out at A New Leash on Love.

That's what she'd given him—a new lease on love.

And now he wanted to give it back again.

Chapter Twelve

"Okay, everyone, roll out." Ruby had backed the family van up to the dog run and was taking barking, whining, overexcited dogs out of their crates as fast as she could manage. She'd spent the better part of the morning at a high-kill shelter and had returned with a selection of eight dogs of various breeds to evaluate for the service-dog program.

Probably only one or two of the eight would have what she was looking for, but she had rescued all of them either way and wouldn't be returning any of these hyperactive pooches to the shelter. Her sisters would work with the ones not selected for the service-dog program on their Canine Good Citizen skills, and hopefully every one of these dogs would be adopted out from A New Leash on Love within a few months.

Every dog was one life saved that otherwise would not be. It made her sad that she couldn't rescue them all, but she did what she could. And right now, her eye was on finding new potential canines for the military veteran program—and in the process, she was trying to keep her mind off Aaron.

It wasn't working.

She kept thinking about where he might be, what he was doing and what his plans for the future were. Had he left town yet? Was he at the airport, headed for a different state, Oscar in tow?

Once she had all the new dogs in the run, she unfolded a chair and sat down with her clipboard to watch the pups interact. Mostly right now, she was allowing them to get out some of their energy before she put them through their paces in an attempt to discover what made each of them tick and how much training each of them may have had.

Were they food motivated, toy motivated or prey motivated? Would she be able to keep their attention, or would they become easily distracted?

She wanted just the right ones to start training for her military contract—that was, assuming she got the contract, which at this point was still up in the air. Now more than ever, she prayed it would go through and that A New Leash on Love would stay afloat. She'd emailed over Aaron's results this morning but hadn't yet heard back from Major Kelley or anyone at her department.

She glanced at her phone to double-check that there were no calls or text messages and once again wondered where Aaron was. Had he already checked out of the bed-and-breakfast?

She could call her sister Avery and ask, she supposed, but Avery and Jake would just tease her incessantly about it, and she had enough on her plate without drawing attention to her futile attraction to Aaron.

Her mind wandered to last night and the wonderful kiss they'd shared. Her whole heart had changed in the blink of an eye when their lips had met. Whatever her feelings, however, Aaron clearly didn't feel the same way. Otherwise, he would have stuck around or at least said something in the moment instead of leaving without a word.

Wouldn't he?

She watched the dogs for a few minutes. All of them had been living in small, cramped kennels, and most hadn't had a bath in weeks. It was no wonder they were acting slaphappy and a little out of control. She would be doing the same if she'd been in such a situation. Her siblings would stop by later in the day to help her give all the pups a sudsy bath before putting them inside nice housing for a change.

It made her smile to know what she could do for them, especially if she was able to help other military men and women such as Aaron in the process. Her heart, which had been aching all day, warmed at the thought. If she couldn't be with Aaron, then at least she could assist his fellow brothers and sisters in arms.

Suddenly, Ruby saw dust from a vehicle rising from down the driveway.

Could it be Aaron?

Had he returned?

Her heart hammered in her head as she waited for the vehicle to round the bend of the barn so she could see it.

It wasn't Aaron.

It was, in fact, an olive green military Hummer with a tall, thin man at the wheel and a dour-looking woman in the passenger seat. She'd never been face-to-face with Major Bren Kelley, but she had no doubt whatsoever in her mind that this woman was she.

Ruby stood and waved. She intended to meet her at the gate and take her into the main training-facility building to show the major around. The new dogs would be safe out here in the yard until she could return to them.

But before she had the opportunity to make it to the gate, Major Kelley was unlatching it and stepping through without first asking.

This surprised Ruby. Most people who weren't familiar with the program's setup would at least wait until they were invited in before stepping into a run chock-full of dogs—and these ones technically weren't even hers yet, until she signed all the papers at the kennel.

As much as she loved dogs, she knew to be cautious in such a situation.

"Ma'am! Ma'am! Please step out of the dog run until I can…"

She raced over to the major and put out her hands, palms up, to stop her, but the major's back was to her, relatching the gate, and she didn't see.

By the time Major Kelley turned around, eight untrained pups were running straight at her, dodging around each other and barking up a storm, trying to be the first to reach and greet her. Three of the dogs ran up to her at once: a loud, baying hound mix; a shepherd-retriever mix; and a medium-sized Heinz 57 dog of undetermined origin.

The hound was louder than the other seven dogs combined, but it was Heinz 57 who really made his presence known, launching from several feet away and landing with his paws squarely across the major's shoulders, upending her onto the ground.

Unfortunately—or perhaps fortunately, depending on the way she looked at it—it had rained the night before, and the major landed directly in the middle of a big mud puddle—probably a much softer landing than she would otherwise have had for her sake but definitely harder on the uniform.

Major Kelley's driver scurried to help her rise to her feet, and Ruby ran to her other side. Together they moved the major out of the dog pen so there wouldn't be any more incidents like the one that had just happened.

This was a full-blown disaster of epic proportions. And if the major's expression was anything to go by, despite her success with Aaron and Oscar, it might very well mean the end of all of Ruby's hard work on the military contract.

Her pulse roared as she attempted to brush mud and dirt from the major's uniform, but it was no use, and Bren soon stepped away with a scoff, lifting her chin imperiously.

"*This* is where I sent my sergeant to be trained?" she demanded. "I was under the impression A New Leash on Love was a professional program, but I can clearly see now that it is not. These dogs are completely unmanageable, and I feel as if I have been severely misled."

"No, ma'am—I mean, yes, ma'am. I can assure you this is a professional program. I didn't have the opportunity to warn you before you entered the dog run unescorted. You've come at the wrong time."

Major Kelley narrowed her eyes on Ruby. "What's that supposed to mean? You expect me to call ahead so you can make your facility look *just so*? Are you trying to pull one over on the military, Ms. Winslow? Because I can assure you that will never work. Lieutenant, hand me my clipboard."

The lieutenant had evidently left the clipboard in the Hummer and dashed off to go get it.

"Please. If you would just let me explain," Ruby begged. "And allow me to show you around the facility. I'm sure after you see—"

"I've already seen more than enough, thank you," the major snapped. "Speak no more of it. I have already made my decision."

The major wasn't even going to listen to reason?

Ruby couldn't help but press on. This whole program depended on her changing the major's mind.

"Didn't you get my email with Aaron's—Sergeant Jamison's—results from the program?" Ruby asked, her voice higher than usual from the strain. "He spent four extremely productive weeks here and passed with flying colors. He is now the proud owner of a service dog, and I can say without a doubt that Oscar is going to be of great help to him going forward. I'm sure if you ask him, he'd agree wholeheartedly."

If she'd known the major would be making an appearance, she would have asked Aaron to stay one more day so Major Kelley could see the end result of the training program. Ruby's heart sank into her gut. All that work, everything she'd done with Aaron, might be for nothing. The major didn't appear to want to listen to reason no matter what she said.

Taking a deep breath and trying not to cry, Ruby turned away and wrapped her arms around herself. She noticed someone else coming down the driveway and hoped they would turn into Winslow's Woodlands and not toward A New Leash on Love. She knew she couldn't handle talking to anyone else today.

Her heart leaped into her throat as she realized it was Aaron's truck coming down the road.

What was he doing here?

She'd thought he was gone without a word, and the fact that he hadn't left town confused her. But his return felt like God's perfect timing. Together with Aaron, she could turn this disaster of a day around. It was critical that she show the major how the program really worked.

Aaron hopped out of the cab with Oscar right on his heel. He'd evidently spotted the major, or at least her vehicle, and wanted to speak with her, but then he noticed Ruby's expression and stopped in his tracks, his boots raising dust.

He made an abrupt turn and approached Ruby instead.

"What's wrong, honey?" he asked, brushing her hair off her face with the tips of his fingers.

Ruby's lips quivered as she fought to keep her emotions under control. "I brought in eight new dogs from a high-kill shelter for evaluation today," she explained. "I'd just arrived back at the farm with them. Obviously,

I had no idea the major was going to show up today, or I would have waited for another time."

"And?"

"I let all the new dogs loose in the dog pen. I thought I'd let them run off some of their energy before I started seriously looking them over and evaluating them for the service-dog program. Ironically, I was especially looking for dogs to work in the new military contract."

She shook her head. "When the major arrived, she let herself into the dog pen before I could stop her. I can't imagine why she did that when she clearly doesn't like canines. If you ask me, she didn't consider her actions. Anyway, three of the new dogs were a bit overenthusiastic and jumped on her. She fell backward into the mud."

"What can I do?"

"Your timing couldn't be more perfect," she admitted. "I was just thinking that if I'd known about the major's visit, I would have asked you to stay one more day. Would you mind showing off your skills?"

A moment later, he was striding toward the major, his steps firm and his shoulders squared, Oscar trotting by his heel.

"Major Kelley?" he called.

"Yes? Who are you?" she demanded.

"Sergeant Aaron Jamison, ma'am." He stood in front of her and saluted, which she promptly returned. "I was the one assigned as the first veteran for A New Leash on Love's military contract."

Her gaze dropped to the poodle by his side, and her eyes widened significantly. "And who is this, Sergeant?" she asked in amazement, clearly already knowing the answer to her question but not believing her eyes.

"This," Aaron said, leaning down to scratch Oscar behind the ears, "is my service dog, Oscar, ma'am."

"You're kidding."

Aaron shook his head and stood back at attention. "No, ma'am. I've been training with Oscar for the past month now and am pleased to report that Oscar and I have successfully passed the program."

The major made an indecipherable noise at the back of her throat but quickly recovered from her amusement.

Somehow, Ruby thought the fact that she had paired a big marine like Aaron with a poodle wasn't a point in her favor any more than a pen full of unruly dogs had been. It was a step in the wrong direction, and she was going downhill fast.

But she wasn't about to give up after working so hard. Now that Aaron was here, she intended to take this back into her own hands.

"I'd like to show you what Aaron has accomplished throughout this program," Ruby said, straightening her shoulders. He was proud of her for stepping up. The major was intimidating.

Aaron squeezed his hands together behind his back. What he really wanted to do was shake the major for not giving Ruby a fair opportunity. From what it looked like to him, Major Kelley had made up her mind from the moment she'd arrived, perhaps before she'd even exited her vehicle. She'd evidently thought the facility ought to look different in some way. Her encounter with the newly recruited dogs had simply sealed the deal.

"Aaron? If you don't mind?" Ruby said.

"Not at all. Come on, Oscar," he coaxed. "Let's do our thing."

Ruby gestured for the major to follow her. "Let's start inside the building," she said. "That way you can examine the inside of the facility while I show you what we do here. I believe you'll find it to be both clean and organized."

Ruby ran ahead to set up a chair for the

major, but Major Kelley walked the perimeter of the inside of the building, taking in the placement and condition of all the equipment before seating herself. Surely, she must have noticed how organized the whole place was and how clean it was, the scent of antiseptic strong in the air.

"When I first arrived, Ruby taught me how to do basic commands with Oscar," he said and then demonstrated.

"We use the clicker to let the dog know the exact moment he has performed the correct command," Ruby added. "If the service dog is motivated by food in the way Oscar is, we follow the clicker with a treat. Different dogs are motivated by different things, such as having a strong prey drive or enjoying their toys."

After Aaron had gone through all the basic commands, he had Oscar sit on one side of the building while he walked all the way over to the other side. He'd become so used to having Oscar beside him to help him balance that he immediately noticed the difference. He concentrated on his walk so he wouldn't stumble.

He was pleased at the expression on Major Kelley's face when Oscar waited for his command and then immediately came to a heel when Aaron called for him. Aaron caught Ruby's gaze and winked in encouragement.

It was going well, but they both knew they weren't finished yet.

Not by a long shot.

Ruby brought him a chair, and he seated himself across from the major, then showed her how Oscar could help him stand when he was having a bad day. Ruby explained how Oscar helped him balance on uneven ground and how he assisted him with forward motion when necessary.

Just to impress the major, Aaron sent Oscar to flip the lights on and off with his muzzle.

Major Kelley's eyes widened, but she didn't say a word.

"It's fairly warm outside today," Ruby told Major Kelley.

Aaron thought perhaps she had been going to say dusty but, given the state of the major's uniform, had decided against it. He was barely able to hold in his amusement.

"I'm parched and I know you must be, as well," Ruby said. "Would you like a bottle of water?"

"Certainly. Thank you."

Aaron gestured for Oscar to head for the refrigerator. As he'd been trained, he opened the door with the attached rope and grabbed a cold bottle of water, returning it to Aaron, who then gestured for Oscar to give it to the major.

This time, Major Kelley spoke. "I've seen military dogs do amazing things, but this is something else entirely."

"Yes, ma'am," he answered, grinning at Ruby. "That he is."

Finally, Ruby asked the major to accompany her out to the agility course—something that Aaron and Oscar had practiced on extensively and then, it turned out, hadn't even been part of the final test. He sent up a grateful prayer to God that he'd taken the extra time on the course. The Lord must have known how he would need it now.

This time Major Kelley didn't enter the pen, even though Oscar was the only dog on the agility course. Instead, she leaned against the fence and watched as Aaron took his place in the middle of the first triangle of obstacles.

"Oscar, *hup*," he called, and the poodle took off toward the first obstacle—the A-frame— at full speed, running up and over with ease, his paws touching the yellow paint on each side, not that the major would be aware of the boundaries Aaron knew, though, and he secretly cheered on his brilliant pup. Then

Oscar swooped into the collapsed tunnel and sailed over the first jump.

By that time, Aaron had already moved into the center of the second three obstacles, and then the last three. When he was finished, he was out of breath, and his lungs were stinging as if he had a hive of wasps in them.

But he'd succeeded.

They had succeeded. He and Oscar, with Ruby's guidance. He and his service dog wouldn't be the team they were without Ruby.

Even the major looked impressed.

He gestured for Ruby to join him and then approached Major Kelley, Oscar back at his heel. Aaron was eager to discover if they'd impressed the major enough to move forward on the contract.

"Do you see what I see?" he asked her. "All that we've accomplished in a mere four weeks, thanks to Ruby Winslow?"

She pursed her lips. "If Ms. Winslow brought you this far in a mere month, then I am impressed. Give me your honest opinion, Sergeant Jamison. Do you think other brothers and sisters in arms will benefit by this program?"

"Yes, ma'am," he said enthusiastically. "I

believe you won't find a better service-dog instructor anywhere than Ruby Winslow."

His heart soared when the major nodded. "I believe you may just be right. And the explanation for the dogs in the yard? I assume there is one." Major Kelley actually chuckled.

Ruby stepped in to answer this question. "Yes, ma'am. There is an explanation for their behavior. They aren't even mine. Or at least, they weren't until today. Just this morning, I took them from a high-kill shelter to evaluate them for my service-dog program. If you come back in a month, you'll see eight completely different dogs, I assure you. If they don't make the service-dog program, I and my siblings will train them to be adopted out to families."

Aaron's heart warmed. He was so proud of Ruby. Even with the rug yanked so painfully out from under her, she held herself erect and didn't give in to the emotions he knew must be flooding through her.

"I owe you an apology," Major Kelley said without preamble. "I judged you without allowing you to show me what you do here. I'm glad you pushed me into seeing the truth. Sergeant Jamison and his dog have displayed amazing growth, and I'm impressed with all Oscar can do for him. The contract is yours."

"I—thank you, Major." Ruby's light blue eyes were glassy, but she didn't cry.

Aaron reached for her hand and threaded his fingers through hers, squeezing gently.

If the major noticed, she didn't comment on it. "Congratulations, Ms. Winslow. I'll get out of your hair now and will be in touch shortly with the paperwork to finalize our contract."

Minutes later, Aaron and Ruby were still standing hand in hand, watching the major's Hummer driving away.

They'd done it.

Contract secured.

But there was one more thing Aaron needed to do before he would rest easy today.

Chapter Thirteen

Ruby turned to Aaron and promptly burst into tears of relief and joy.

"Hey, now," Aaron said, opening his arms to her. "Shh, baby. What's all this about?"

She stepped into his embrace and buried her face in his shoulder as he gently and silently stroked her back. He felt so solid and warm as she clung to him, and she never wanted to let go.

Everything had been on the verge of completely falling apart at the seams for a while there. She'd held it together while the major had been there, but now all the emotions she'd held in check were threatening to overwhelm her.

And Aaron had shown up at just the right time.

"I thought for a moment there I was going

to lose everything," she said, leaning back and wiping her wet cheeks with her palms.

"What are you talking about? You opened Major Kelley's eyes today. If it weren't for you, I'd still be all alone in the world, feeling sorry for myself instead of having a wonderful companion service dog to help me through life."

He framed her face with his large hands. "Make no mistake about it," he said, capturing her gaze, "you deserve this contract. You've worked hard for it. And you're going to do wonderful things in the future for my brothers and sisters in arms, as much as you've done for me. I believe in you."

She'd thought she'd had her tears under control, but she started sobbing again at his tender words. He held her and let her cry as she released all the emotions and tensions this day had brought upon her.

"What would I do without you?" she murmured into his shirt.

Clearing his throat, he glanced at the ground and dug the toe of his boot into the earth. "Yeah, about that…"

He paused and she stopped breathing, leaning back to look up at him.

"What would you say if I stuck around for a while?"

"Around Whispering Pines? Are you serious?" Her pulse was roaring.

He wasn't leaving!

"You want to stay?" she asked, almost afraid she'd heard wrong.

He shrugged. "Only if you want me to."

Did she ever. She couldn't think of anything she wanted more.

"I've already got a good side hustle going."

"Really?" It probably would have been easier for them to speak if they stepped apart, but there was no way Ruby was going to let that happen. Her arms remained firmly around his neck and his were equally strong around her waist.

"I spent the morning in town speaking with Sally at the pizza joint and Doug at his ice-cream shop."

"Is that right? So, will you be delivering pizzas or scooping ice cream?" she teased, not caring what he did as long as it meant he was staying.

"Neither. I was hawking my cupcakes."

"Seriously? Oh, Aaron, that's wonderful. I'm so proud of you."

His face reddened under her scrutiny, but his smile couldn't have been wider.

"For the moment, it's a part-time gig, but I wanted to show you I'm a man who can provide for his family and not the total washout I was when I first arrived in town."

"What do you plan to do with the rest of your time?" she asked curiously.

He bent his head down toward hers and captured her gaze with his. "I've really gotten into this whole dog-training thing. What you do here is nothing short of phenomenal, and I would be honored to be a part of it. I know this isn't usually how a job interview is supposed to go, but I was really hoping you might offer me something here. I'd like to work for you. I'm not picky. I'll clean up the dog pens and feed the pups or whatever you need me to do."

Ruby wanted to pinch herself. Hours earlier, her heart had been broken and her future looked lonely at best. Now she was standing in Aaron's arms, listening to his wonderful plans for the future.

A future that included her.

"Of course, you can come work with me. *With* me, Aaron, not for me. I can't think of anything I'd like better," she said without missing a beat. "I thought you'd left for good. I so wanted to ask you to stay," she said, her tears coming back in earnest now.

"Then why didn't you?"

"Because you disappeared right after we'd

shared our kiss together. And I thought that meant you didn't want to be with me."

He shook his head. "Are you kidding? There's nowhere else I'd rather be than right here. Don't you know what you've done for me?"

She shook her head.

"I thought I was no good to the world. I believed my life was over because I could no longer serve in the marines. You showed me there is so much more to life. You forced me to look beyond myself and my problems because you needed me to help you secure your military contract. And because you never abandoned me, you didn't allow me to lose hope about myself. Your service-dog program is perfectly named. You've given me a new lease on love, Ruby, and I'll never be able to repay you for that. I'd like to try, though."

She chuckled through her tears, her heart feeling as if it would burst in her chest. "That's really sweet."

He grinned and touched his forehead to hers. "I wasn't aiming for sweet."

"No?" Her voice softened. "What, then?"

"I taught Oscar a new trick, one that isn't part of the program. Do you want to see it?"

"If you want to show it to me," she said. It seemed to her to be a strange time to bring up a dog trick, and she wondered if he was emotionally backing off again. It wouldn't be the first time that had happened.

He blocked Oscar from view for a moment as he leaned over him. When he stood to his full height again, his smile had left his face and his gaze was unreadable.

"Check it out," he said, gesturing toward Oscar, who approached Ruby, carefully balancing a sparkling—

Was it a diamond solitaire on his muzzle?

Oscar sat handsomely without disturbing the ring at all.

Ruby was in shock. She couldn't move or breath or—*anything*.

Aaron picked up the ring off Oscar's muzzle and took her right hand in his. His smile returned as he placed her palm over his heart.

"I—I can't kneel," he said. "Even though I really want to. I'm kneeling in my heart, okay?"

Ruby hiccuped a sob and nodded as tears flooded into her eyes and down her cheeks.

"You're amazing, you know that?" he said, his voice even lower and raspier than usual. "I've known for some time that I had serious feelings for you, but the night at the bonfire when we kissed sealed the deal for me."

"Me, too," she whispered.

"I can't live without you. Being needed by someone is a whole new experience for me. You've opened up my whole world. Now I want to give it back to you. I love you more than I ever believed I could love someone. You're *my* whole world, Ruby. Will you marry me?"

Her left hand shook as she offered it to Aaron, and he slid the ring onto her finger. Then he leaned down and tenderly kissed her, sealing their promise.

"This part isn't going into the service-dog program," he murmured.

She giggled. "I love you, you big grumpy marine. This is definitely a one of a kind."

"Yes, it is." His voice was thick with emotion. "Our new leash on love."

"Our new leash on love," she echoed before his lips touched hers again, making everything right in their world.

Epilogue

Two Years Later

Aaron had been working hard all morning on a batch of cupcakes—one cupcake in particular. He'd been a married man for a year now and couldn't be happier with his wife, Ruby, and their service-dog program. He still provided cupcakes for Sally's Pizza and the ice-cream shop, as well as Winslow's Woodlands gift shop.

He and Ruby had built a cabin on Winslow land, and he spent most of his time working with service dogs, especially for the military veterans who regularly came in due to the contract Ruby had obtained.

He probably didn't have to keep baking cupcakes, but he enjoyed being able to put the extra money into a college fund for any children they might have.

What had once been saving for the future had now become much more of a reality when, about four and a half months ago, Ruby discovered they were pregnant. It had been a surprise to them both, but they couldn't have been happier.

Aaron sometimes felt as if he should pinch himself, wondering how he'd come from being a wounded marine with no future at all to a happily married man with a growing family, and—well, that was a surprise, too.

He and Ruby had gone in for the reveal ultrasound just yesterday. Ruby wasn't yet aware of the ultrasound results. Aaron wouldn't even let her look at the monitor.

Aaron had suddenly come up with an idea that he thought would make Ruby happy and had asked her sisters to help him plan and execute a surprise for her. He still thanked God every day for gracing him with the Winslows' large brood. Not having had any brothers or sisters growing up and feeling completely isolated as an adult was a thing of the past. Now he had siblings galore and as much help as he needed to make this one of the happiest days of his beloved wife's life.

Today, the whole family would be gathering for a picnic, where Ruby would get to find out in the midst of her loved ones who she was expecting.

Before yesterday, they'd gone back and forth about the possible gender of their child. Ruby was convinced she was carrying Aaron's son, but in Aaron's heart of hearts, he wanted a daughter who was as beautiful and precious as his wife. Sure, teaching a boy to throw a ball would be fun, but he could teach his daughter the same thing, and he'd learned a lot about tea parties from Lottie.

At present, he was the only one who knew the results of the ultrasound. He hadn't even shared it with any of Ruby's sisters, figuring they'd all enjoy finding out at one time. He was in charge of the cupcake, and he'd carefully added the cream to the middle. It was yellow cake with mint-green frosting on the outside. Not only was mint green a neutral color and could convincingly be considered a baby theme, but it reminded him of another time and place and a gorgeous redhead with mint-green frosting in her hair.

Hopefully, this cupcake would truly be the best one she'd ever tasted.

Ruby couldn't decide if she was more nervous or excited. Definitely a lot of both. Butterflies had loosed in her stomach, and her adrenaline had kicked in with a vengeance—making her baby do loop-de-loops and jumping jacks in her womb. Goodness, but he was an active little guy.

Or girl, as Aaron was so fond of reminding her.

She dressed in her maternity jeans and a top that would have worked for a tent. She couldn't believe how much she'd grown over the past five months. One would think she was carrying an elephant if they didn't know better. Yet one more reason why she believed she was carrying Aaron's son, a big boy who'd grow into a large man like her handsome husband.

And speaking of her husband—he'd certainly grown tight-lipped. She knew he and her sisters were planning a reveal party. They could hardly keep that a secret since Aaron wouldn't even let her see the ultrasound that she'd so been looking forward to watching. Thankfully, he promised he'd had a disc made of it and they'd get to watch it together as soon as the party was over.

"Almost ready to go, babe?" Aaron asked, buttoning up the same black shirt he'd worn the first night they'd kissed.

She walked over to him and wrapped her

arms around his neck, playfully jerking at his collar. "Do you remember the first time you wore this?"

He snorted. "How could I forget? The tag was still attached to the shirt. How embarrassing."

"And yet, as I seem to recall, you got over it."

"I remember." His raspy voice had lowered, along with his head, as he brushed his lips across hers.

She framed his face in her hands, enjoying the same light scruff that she'd felt under her palms that first night. "When I kissed you the night of the bonfire, I thought I'd made a mistake. I tried to pull away."

"Mmm. I wasn't going to let you do that, now, was I?"

"Thankfully not. I love you, sweetie."

He growled, as he always did when she blessed him with that moniker. A marine, he'd told her on several occasions, was not sweet.

"I love you, too. Now let's get going. Your family is waiting for us, and if I'm not mistaken, they're nearly as anxious as you are to find out what we're having. I foresee a lot of shopping in the near future."

Ruby was definitely looking forward to

baby shopping. She'd been window-shopping for tiny clothing for months now. It was hard to believe she'd be holding her own baby in just a matter of months.

Even though the picnic table was a fairly easy walk from their cabin, Aaron made her take their truck, which was its own obstacle, as getting her unwieldy body into the cab wasn't exactly an easy thing to do—at least until Aaron swept her into his arms and deposited her on the passenger seat. He totally spoiled her.

And she liked it.

When they pulled up to the picnic site, Jake and Avery's Lottie and Molly and Logan's Judah were swinging on the nearby play set while Jake and Avery helped now almost three-year-old Felix slide down the slide.

Felicity, Molly and Logan were setting up the table with sandwiches and chips, including Felicity's specialty vegan courses. Felicity had become vegan during her college years, and though her siblings liked to tease her about it, they always made sure she had plenty to eat at family gatherings. A canvas chair had been set up for her grandfather, and he was happily snoozing in the shade. Sharpe was sitting on the cooler that held bottles of water, regaling the clan with a story about one of the recent customers to the tree farm. Frost had already pulled out his guitar and was strumming a tune.

Aaron helped Ruby out of the cab of the truck and then grabbed a canvas chair from the back and hurried to open it for her, not contented until she was comfortably off her feet.

"You've got a good one there," Felicity teased. "Look how he takes care of you as if you were a china doll."

"He'd better," Sharpe said, tipping his bottle of water toward Aaron. "Unless he wants Frost and me to do a number on him."

"Ooh, scary," Aaron said, shaking his head.

"Be afraid," Sharpe teased back. "Be very afraid."

"Are we going to do the reveal before or after we eat?" Felicity asked excitedly. "I vote before, if anyone wants to know."

"After," said Sharpe and Frost at the same time.

"Now, why did I figure they'd say that?" Ruby asked. "Are you trying to make me expire from anticipation?"

"Better than expiring from lack of food," Jake said, sitting down at the table.

"Men. Honestly. I think we'd better pass

out the sandwiches," Felicity said with a dramatic sigh.

As much as Ruby wanted to get to the good part, she knew she wouldn't have the men's complete attention until their stomachs were full.

She, on the other hand, couldn't eat more than a couple of bites, she was so excited. She was always hungry these days, but this was an exception to the rule. She nibbled small bites of her sandwich and waited for the others to finish eating. Fortunately, with the guys, it didn't take long for them to wolf down their lunches.

"*Now* can we do the reveal?" Felicity said, her hands on her hips. "And if anyone makes another excuse, I'm going to send them home without letting them get to find out the good news."

And it *would* be good news—boy or girl.

Ruby was shaking so hard she wasn't sure she could hold the cupcake in her hand when Aaron finally handed it to her.

"Mint-green frosting," she exclaimed in delight, pressing her free palm to her heart. "You remembered."

"Hard to forget. You had it in your hair." Aaron and Jake burst into laughter, and the rest of Ruby's siblings looked at them with interest.

"This sounds like a story," Frost said.

"For another time," Felicity said, waving a dishcloth at him. "Can we please focus on Ruby's cupcake here?"

Ruby was all in agreement for that.

"Ready?" she asked, holding the cupcake to her lips.

Felicity squealed. "More than…"

"Let's count 'er down," Aaron suggested. "And three…two…one…"

Ruby took a bite of the cupcake and then stared down in surprise and confusion.

"Aaron?" she asked, glancing up at her grinning husband. "I don't understand."

She had been expecting blue filling inside the cupcake.

Or pink. She would have been equally happy with pink.

But it was neither.

Aaron pressed a gentle hand to her tummy. "Do you want to know why you feel so much activity in here?"

"Enlighten me," she said, displaying the inside of the cupcake for all her brothers and sisters to see.

The filling was purple.

Aaron's eyes were shining.

Purple.

Not pink.

Not blue.

But when Aaron had mixed the two together…

Despite her usual difficulty rising from her seat, she launched herself into Aaron's arms, tears running down her face.

"What?" her grandfather said, suddenly coming awake. "What is it?"

"I'm not positive about this," Felicity told him, "but I think Ruby and Aaron are having…"

A smiling, crying Ruby and proud papa Aaron finished the statement for her.

"Twins!"

* * * * *

Dear Reader,

How wonderful to be at the midpoint of my series Rocky Mountain Family, starring the six Winslow siblings who live and work on a Christmas tree farm and service-dog rescue in the fictional town of Whispering Pines, Colorado. I'm so enjoying writing a happily-ever-after for each Winslow sibling located in my home state. I hope you enjoy these tales— or should I say tails?

In this book, you'll meet Oscar, a black standard poodle with a teddy bear cut who is being trained to help grumpy Sergeant Aaron Jamison, who was injured in battle. He wants nothing to do with a froufrou dog and immediately butts heads with his trainer, Ruby Winslow. What a lovely story of redemption this turned out to be, and I hope you enjoy reading it as much as I enjoyed writing it.

I'm always delighted to hear from you, dear readers, and I love to connect socially. To get regular updates, please visit my website and sign up for my newsletter at https://www.debkastnerbooks.com. Come join me on Facebook at DebKastnerBooks, and/or catch me on Twitter @debkastner.

Please know that I pray for each and every one of you daily.

Dare to Dream,
Deb Kastner

Get 4 FREE REWARDS!

We'll send you 2 FREE Books plus 2 FREE Mystery Gifts.

Love Inspired Suspense books showcase how courage and optimism unite in stories of faith and love in the face of danger.

FREE
Value Over
$20

YES! Please send me 2 FREE Love Inspired Suspense novels and my 2 FREE mystery gifts (gifts are worth about $10 retail). After receiving them, if I don't wish to receive any more books, I can return the shipping statement marked "cancel." If I don't cancel, I will receive 6 brand-new novels every month and be billed just $5.24 each for the regular-print edition or $5.99 each for the larger-print edition in the U.S., or $5.74 each for the regular-print edition or $6.24 each for the larger-print edition in Canada. That's a savings of at least 13% off the cover price. It's quite a bargain! Shipping and handling is just 50¢ per book in the U.S. and $1.25 per book in Canada.* I understand that accepting the 2 free books and gifts places me under no obligation to buy anything. I can always return a shipment and cancel at any time. The free books and gifts are mine to keep no matter what I decide.

Choose one: ☐ **Love Inspired Suspense Regular-Print**
(153/353 IDN GNWN)

☐ **Love Inspired Suspense Larger-Print**
(107/307 IDN GNWN)

Name (please print)

Address   Apt. #

City   State/Province   Zip/Postal Code

Email: Please check this box ☐ if you would like to receive newsletters and promotional emails from Harlequin Enterprises ULC and its affiliates. You can unsubscribe anytime.

Mail to the **Harlequin Reader Service:**
IN U.S.A.: P.O. Box 1341, Buffalo, NY 14240-8531
IN CANADA: P.O. Box 603, Fort Erie, Ontario L2A 5X3

Want to try 2 free books from another series! Call 1-800-873-8635 or visit www.ReaderService.com.

LIS21R

Get 4 FREE REWARDS!

We'll send you 2 FREE Books <u>plus</u> 2 FREE Mystery Gifts.

Harlequin Heartwarming Larger-Print books will connect you to uplifting stories where the bonds of friendship, family and community unite.

FREE Value Over $20

HARLEQUIN SELECTS COLLECTION

19 FREE BOOKS IN ALL!

From Robyn Carr to RaeAnne Thayne to Linda Lael Miller and Sherryl Woods we promise (actually, GUARANTEE!) each author in the Harlequin Selects collection has seen their name on the *New York Times* or *USA TODAY* bestseller lists!